THE
RING

For Madison,
who never, ever gives up on her dreams.

THE RING

Bobbie Pyron

WestSide Books
Lodi, New Jersey

Published by WestSide Books
60 Industrial Road
Lodi, NJ 07644
973-458-0485
Fax: 973-458-5289

Library of Congress Control Number: 2009930785

International Standard Book Number: 978-1-934813-09-6
School ISBN: 978-1-934813-25-6
Cover design by David Lemanowicz
Interior design by David Lemanowicz

Printed in Canada
10 9 8 7 6 5 4 3 2 1

First Edition

THE
RING

ONE

Okay, here's number one on the top-ten list of signs you've totally screwed up: riding in the back of a cop car at one in the morning.

The definition of pissed: the look on your dad's face when he comes to bail you out.

A cop handed Dad a clipboard. "Mr. Wolfe, we need your signature on these forms before we can release your daughter."

Dad flipped through the papers, shaking his head. "Isn't this just great? My fifteen-year-old daughter's been charged with drunken and disorderly conduct."

Officer Clipboard shrugged. "Happens, sir."

I wanted to say, "Don't mind me while I go slit my wrists," but I didn't.

Dad paced back and forth. "What were you thinking, Mardie? What ever possessed you to sneak out in the middle of the night and get drunk?"

I slumped lower on the hard wooden stool, head pounding and stomach churning.

What did he want me to say? It seemed like a good idea when Ben called? Ben Richter—the hottest senior at school—called *me* in that low, sexy voice. "Come on, Mardie. Come on out and play." It felt so good to have someone like Ben want to be with someone like me.

Dad stood over me, tapping his pen on the clipboard. He pushed his glasses up on his nose like he does when he's lecturing at the college. "What's going on with you, Mardie? It's been one thing after another lately."

He ticked off my offenses on his fingers. "First you dyed your blond hair this ugly Goth black. Then your grades went down the toilet. And now this mess."

I said something lame like, "I don't know, Dad. I just didn't think . . ."

"You're damn right you didn't think!" Dad's face was crimson. That little vein in his temple jumped. Both are sure signs he's about to blow.

Then, just like a scene out of a really bad movie, my cell phone rang. I grabbed my phone out of my pocket and flipped it open.

Dad thrust his hand under my nose. "Hand it over, Mardie."

"But Dad, just let me—"

"Hand it over now, or I'll answer that call myself."

Shit. I handed him the phone.

Officer Clipboard returned. He handed Dad some papers. He looked at me and then spoke to Dad. "You understand, if she gets caught doing something like this again, she'll have to go to juvie court."

Dad crammed the papers in his coat pocket. "Don't

worry, Officer. She won't be going anywhere again until she's thirty."

Cold sweat popped out on my arms. The buzz of the fluorescent light drilled into the side of my head. I jerked my hair up off my neck. I wished Dad would stop yelling and pacing and just take me home.

"I don't feel so good, Dad," I moaned.

"You're going to feel a hell of a lot worse when—"

Then I puked on his shoes.

When we got home, I crawled into bed and cried myself to sleep like some baby. And then I dreamed about my mother. In my dream I was crying and scared, trapped in a dark closet with no way out. As I cried and beat my fists against the walls, I felt cool, soft hands stroke my arms and my tangled, sweaty hair. In this little-girl voice I said, "I don't feel so good, Mommy." A voice floated down from above, saying, "You'll be all right, sweetie-pie. Everything will be just . . ."

Sunshine slapped my face. "Get up," snapped my step-mom, Amy, flinging open the bedroom curtains. "Your dad wants to talk to you in the kitchen."

"Can't I talk to him later?" I whined, burrowing under my comforter.

Amy pulled back the covers. "Sorry, Mardie. You make your bed, you lie in it. After that stunt you pulled last night, you're lucky it's me coming in to get you up and not your dad."

Amy glared at the window screen I'd popped out last night. She shook her head, muttered something I couldn't hear.

"Five minutes, young lady. You've got five minutes to get yourself out of that bed and into the kitchen."

I dug some sweats and my brother's old T-shirt out of a pile of clothes on the floor. The T-shirt looked like the dogs had chewed it, but on the front it said MEAN PEOPLE SUCK. Maybe Dad would get a clue.

I shuffled down the hallway to the kitchen. As I passed Dad's study, I heard his voice through the open door.

"Yeah, Dad, I'm fine. Just tired. I was up late grading papers. They have me teaching two freshman history sections this year. Kids are fine. Michael's great. Did I tell you he's captain of the lacrosse team this year? Yeah, we're proud. He's sending off for college catalogs and checking out different programs on the Web. His grades are super. He should have his pick of colleges."

All this talk about my older brother, Michael the Great, made me feel even more nauseated. Especially when Dad said, "Oh, I expect he'll go into history just like me. That kid and I are like two peas in a pod."

Dad sighed. "Mardie's okay, I guess. She's got all that teenage-girl stuff going on. I tell you, Dad, girls are a lot harder. Sometimes I don't think I even know her anymore."

A sliver of sadness stabbed my heart.

Then Dad said, "Sometimes I worry she's just a little too much like her mother."

That made me want to smash something. Wasn't that always the way it was? Michael is oh-so-perfect. Michael is just like him. Me, I'm "just like" my mother. A person he never talks about except in anger, except in disappointment, and especially when I screw up. Why do I have to be "just like" anybody? Can't I be just like me?

I ran into my best friend Alexis on my way to the cafeteria on Monday. We've known each other since forever. She's like this little elf with wild gypsy hair. In the last year, I've really shot up and filled out. Most of the time it's kind of cool to be tall as Dad. But next to Alexis, I feel like the Incredible Hulk.

"Hey," she said. "I tried calling you all day yesterday. But your parents wouldn't let me talk to you. Even Michael said"—and here Alexis did a perfect imitation of my brother's snotty, superior voice—"'Sorry little friend, but Mardie's in the seventh circle of hell.'"

I laughed. Alexis can always make me laugh. In my book that's right up there on the top-ten list of what you want in a best friend.

"Yeah, I 'displayed poor judgment' and snuck out to a party." We elbowed our way into the cafeteria. "A bunch of kids showed up with beer, things got a little crazy and I ended up at the police station. The Professor definitely was not pleased."

A Latina girl shoved past us, knocking Alexis with her lunch tray.

"Watch it," I snapped.

The girl looked over her shoulder and sang out, "Sorry! My bad!"

I started to say something when Alexis grabbed my wrist.

"Keep your mouth shut, Mardie," she said, "and let's just get a table."

"Why? What's the deal?"

Alexis whispered almost comically behind her hand. "I heard she *boxes*, Mardie. Like you see on TV."

I glanced over. The girl sorted her aluminum from her plastics at the recycle bins. "She looks pretty harmless to me."

"She's Hispanic and she fights. Who knows? She might carry a knife or something."

I laughed. "Give me a break, Al," I said. "You've been watching too much TV."

We passed the Jock Table, the Cheerleader Table, and the Suffering Artists Table. We found empty seats by the windows with the other kids who don't quite fit in anywhere else. No one ever said high school is democratic.

I checked the Jock Table for Ben. No sign of him there. The last I saw of him at the party, he executed an amazing vault over the deck railing and took off into the night.

Alexis said, "I heard about that party from Sam. I wanted to go, but there was no way I could get past my mom's radar. How did you pull it off?"

"Just popped the screen out of my bedroom window."

Alexis shook her head. "You're a lot braver than I am. How'd you get over to Sam's?"

I smiled. "Guess."

She leaned forward, eyes even wider. "Ohmigod Ben?"

I grinned like I had the answer to the million-dollar question. "You got it."

She shook her head and said, "How could you *not* go. I mean, *Ben Richter*."

Alexis unwrapped her sandwich, lifted the top piece of bread, and sniffed. Here we were in tenth grade, and her mom still made her lunch every day.

"Yeah, Sam filled me in on what happened at his house, the cops showing up and all. What did your parents do?"

I scanned the cafeteria again for Ben. Where was he anyway?

"They were pretty freaked. I got the Mardie-We-Just-Don't-Understand-You speech, followed by taking my cell phone away and grounding me for god knows how long."

Alexis wadded her paper bag. "Sam's parents are totally freaking out. They're talking about sending him to military school!"

I bet Dad would love to send me to military school, turn me into a perfect little robot who acts, thinks, and talks just like everybody else.

I narrowed one eye and lobbed Alexis's lunch bag into the trash can. Nothing but net.

That afternoon, I rode the city bus two stops past our neighborhood. The rules for being grounded were: 1. no going anywhere after school except home, and 2. no leaving the house once I got there. I figured I was more or less following the rules. I was allowed to have one friend over when I was grounded, which normally would have been Alexis. But she'd joined everything from the drama club to the debate team since we'd started tenth grade—her way of trying to fit in—so she rarely had time to just hang out after school.

As for me, until I met Ben, it'd never really mattered about fitting in. As long as I had soccer, and horses, and Alexis, I didn't care about much else. Even in ninth grade, I didn't worry too much. Nobody cared about ninth-graders anyway—the bottom feeders in the high school social food chain.

But last summer Alexis got interested in Sam, and he's friends with Ben. And since where Alexis goes, I go, too, I went swimming with her at the quarry in August. That's when I met up with Ben, with that lazy, crooked smile.

I stopped at the Shop-N-Go for something sweet and gooey. Amy was on another one of her health food crusades, and Dad was trying to lose weight. That meant there wasn't anything remotely worth eating in the house.

I wandered down the rows of candy, chips, and cookies, trying to decide between Pixie Stix and a Snickers, watching the clerk out of the corner of my eye. When she turned her back to grab a pack of cigarettes for a biker guy, I slipped the Snickers in my sweatshirt pocket. By the time I got to the end of our driveway, my heart was still beating a zillion miles an hour. *What a freakin' rush!* I peeled back the wrapper and bit into the chocolatey, gooey mess.

I finally saw Ben after school a few days later, on the way out the door.

"I thought the 'rents sent you to outer Siberia or something," I said.

Ben grinned and draped an arm across my shoulders. I swear I could feel his heat burning right through my sweater.

"Nah, just laying low for a couple of days. My mom was totally whacked about the whole thing. Threatened to keep me off the basketball team."

Ben steered me through the sea of kids rushing to cars and school buses.

"So what happened?" I asked.

"Dad basically said 'boys will be boys.' He had to do something, though, so Mom'd get off our backs. So he took away my car keys for two weeks. Hence," he said as the city bus pulled up to the stop, "the public transportation."

The bus doors folded open. Ben bowed, sweeping his arm wide. "Your chariot awaits, fair maiden." When Ben smiled at me like that, his gray eyes all crinkly in the corners, with his sexy uneven front teeth, little fishes jumped in my veins.

We took the bus into town, and grabbed a couple of drinks at Starbucks. It was one of those amazing fall days we get in the foothills of the Rockies: warm sun, crisp air, a sky so blue, it makes your eyes hurt. And Ben Richter right beside me, laughing and making stupid jokes. Who cared if I was supposed to go straight home after school?

Who cared if I was getting these what's-a-nobody-like-you-doing-with-someone-like-Ben looks from everybody from school. Life just didn't get any better.

Ben and I wandered down King Street. South Eden, like a lot of small mountain towns in Colorado, was a big mining center a long time ago. Most of the streets are named for either mines or tragically killed miners. And our high school football team is named—you guessed it—The Mighty Miners.

We rounded King Street and came to Rossi Court. A tall iron gate opened to the town cemetery. I froze and my throat tightened.

"Let's go find a nice cozy spot," Ben said.

"I don't really want to. Let's just catch the bus and ride around."

But Ben slipped an arm around me, drawing me close. There went those damn little fish again. "Come on, Mar. It's almost Halloween. What better time to take a stroll around the graveyard? I promise I'll keep you safe."

We walked under the spreading limbs of bare trees, with headstones that marched in straight rows as far as we could see. For a small town, we sure had a lot of dead people.

I held tight to Ben, trying not to look at the headstones, and forcing myself to focus on his words as he made fun of the inscriptions chiseled in the hard, cold granite.

Ben pointed to a small marker. "Hey, look over here. There's someone with your last name."

I walked over, my palms sweating. This was the last thing I'd wanted to see.

"See, Mar? It says 'Erin Wolfe.' The last name is even spelled the same."

I squeezed my eyes shut, willing tears to stay put.

"You okay?" Ben asked.

"I don't feel all that great. I think I better go home."

He studied my face. "Is she a relative or something?"

"Yeah. She's my mother."

Ben's face softened. No stupid jokes this time. He pulled me to him and I buried my face in his leather coat. He stroked my hair, saying, "Christ, Mardie, I'm sorry. I had no idea. What an ass. . . ."

I pulled back and looked up at him. "It's okay, Ben. I was only four when she died. I really don't even remember her."

Then I let myself look at the headstone and the chiseled words that read:

ERIN MARIE WOLFE

BELOVED MOTHER, WIFE, AND FRIEND

LOVED MUCH. TAKEN TOO SOON

If we didn't leave fast, I was going to lose it. I grabbed Ben's warm, living hand and said, "Come on."

"Must be weird not having a mother," Ben said as we waited for my bus. I shrugged.

"I mean, my mom drives me nuts most of the time, but I wouldn't want her to die or anything." He brushed the hair away from my face. "What's it like having a dead mother, Mar?"

A white vapor trail cut across the perfect blue sky. "I don't know," I said. "It's not really *like* anything. And as I told you back there, I don't really remember her at all."

Before he could get any more sensitive on me, my bus pulled up. I kissed him quickly on the cheek, and said, "Gotta get home."

He shot me that two-hundred-watt smile. "Well, all I can say is your mom must have been one hot lady, judging by the way you turned out."

My knees went all rubbery. And I'm sure my face turned baboon's-butt red. That was more like the Ben I knew.

No sign of the folks when I got home—just Michael's old VW in the driveway.

Teddy and Max, our two dogs, danced around my legs as I took off my jacket.

"I thought you were grounded," Michael said, using his superior, big-brother voice.

"So what's your point?" I retorted, throwing Max's favorite squeaky toy down the hall.

I sat at the breakfast bar and watched Michael make a sandwich. But it would be more accurate to say he constructed it: first came a thick layer of extra-crunchy peanut butter on a piece of Amy's industrial-strength homemade bread. Then came thin slices of apple, followed by a smooth film of jelly. He topped the whole thing off with crumbled potato chips and the final slice of bread. It was an architectural wonder.

"You're so weird, Michael," I said.

"It all ends up in the same place," he mumbled around a huge bite. "I'm just being efficient."

I got a Coke from the fridge and watched him eat. Finally, I asked him, "Do you remember Mom?"

Michael was quiet for a second. "Not a whole lot, Mardie. I was only six when she died." Teddy's pleading eyes followed the sandwich.

"Tell me whatever you remember."

Michael chewed, staring off into space. "I remember that every spring, she'd sing to the tulips and daffodils. And she told us stories in the morning while Dad made us breakfast."

"What kind of stories?" I pressed.

"Like what our stuffed animals did during the night while we were asleep. They'd wake her up needing drinks of water, stuff like that."

My heart ached.

"She sounds wonderful," I said. "Why won't Dad talk about her?"

Michael frowned. "She and Dad fought a lot. She'd go storming out, and sometimes she wouldn't come home at night."

We were both quiet.

Then Michael asked, "Do you remember much about her? You were what, four, when she died?"

I sighed. "No, I don't really remember her, except for her hands for some reason. I just remember her hands."

Two

A few nights later, as I chopped carrots for a salad, Amy said, "Your dad and Michael have an away game for lacrosse on Friday, so they won't be home until Saturday night sometime."

"So?" I said.

"*So*, I have my Tai Chi class on Friday night. Since no one else will be here, you'll be coming with me to the gym."

"Geez Amy, can't I just stay home and watch a movie or something? You'll only be gone a couple of hours, right?"

Amy tossed a handful of onions in the skillet. "Nope, honey, you can't. We just can't trust you right now."

"But I give you my word—I won't do anything," I said, tracing an X over my heart.

She wiped her hands on a dish towel I made in Girl Scouts. "Sorry, Mardie," she said. "You're going to have to work pretty hard to convince us your *word* means something again."

Later that night, I lay on my bedroom floor, all the lights off, stroking the soft top of Max's head. I stared up at the glow-in-the-dark universe that was scattered across my ceiling. Dad and I had this yearly ritual: on the night of the winter solstice, we take down the old, peeling stars and planets and replace them with a sparkly new set. The shooting stars were my favorite.

The solstice was almost two months away. My stars were fading, and their arms were curling in on themselves. A few of the planets had fallen off, leaving me incomplete solar systems. Reminded me of my life.

The radio on my night table was tuned to KPEL. That's the radio station where Michael works, one of those FM stations way down at the end of the dial, where you're likely to hear almost anything. One guy plays nothing newer than 1950s music. Another girl plays weird things like native chanting from Micronesia or symphonies written for didgeridoos, that weird Australian aboriginal horn, or else chirping crickets or worse. But tonight was Michael's night on air.

Max lay there asleep, his feet twitching as he snored. As I drifted off myself, I wondered what dogs dream about.

But in my own dream, I was at the ocean. I heard the screech of seagulls overhead as waves pounded the shore. And though the sun was shining, for some reason my vision was dark, and oddly out of focus. If I could only open my eyes a little wider, I'd be able to find what I was searching for. Then suddenly a huge wave rose above me, getting higher and scarier as it swelled. I looked around wildly and cried, "Mommy! Mommy!" The wave towered over me and I tried hard to run but wet sand sucked my feet deeper with every step. Just as I started to scream, my mother's hands reached out to me. They were soft and strong, with something shining on one hand. I wondered how she could hold a hot, bright star on her finger.

But then I woke with a start. I climbed into bed and pulled the covers over my head, trying my best to wish back that last part of my dream. But that's the thing about dreams: the harder you try to hang on to them, the slipperier they become.

There were a surprising number of cars in the parking lot at the gym Friday night when Amy and I pulled in. What were all these people doing at the city gym on a Friday night, for chrissakes? Didn't they have anything better to do?

I slouched in behind Amy, still pissed that I had to come with her at all. Amy suggested I join her Tai Chi class (*oh, yeah, right*) or bring a book to read. So now I had two hours of excruciating boredom on my hands. At least if I were home, I could talk to Ben on the house phone, since Amy and Dad still have my cell.

I wandered past the other classrooms in the gym. Squeaking tennis shoes on hardwood floors came from the basketball court. I used to be pretty good at basketball, even soccer, too. But it seemed like the older I got, the less appealing being a "team player" became.

Music throbbed from another room, where a shrill female voice commanded, "Harder! Everybody! Peddle harder!" A spinning class. The room was packed.

More music and rhythmic pounding pulled me to the far end of the gym hallway. I walked down to the source of the sounds and looked in.

The room was alive with strong-looking women. Some were dancing around duffle-shaped hanging bags, pummeling the hell out of them. Others jumped rope so fast, the rope seemed to blur.

A Latina girl batted at a small, lightbulb-shaped bag hanging in the doorway. She glanced my way and smiled, missing a beat. I blinked. She was that girl in the school cafeteria the other day.

I backed away and wandered farther down the hall. What I saw through a glass wall totally nailed my feet to the floor. There in the boxing ring were two women, wearing helmets and huge gloves. They danced around each other, rocking from one foot to another, their hands tucked in close to their chins.

A black woman called from the side of the ring, "Come on, ladies, mix it up! Stop fighting like a couple of girls!"

The one in bright red shorts shot out her arm, nailing the other in the side of her helmet, making her stagger backward.

"Gloves up, Chris," the woman called from ringside.

Chris shook her head, then regained her balance. She dipped one shoulder and hooked her other arm up, slamming her fist hard against the taller woman's helmet.

"That's more like it. Good job!" the woman said. "That's enough for now. Give me fifty crunches, then hit the showers."

The two women removed their helmets. The taller woman gave the other one a slap on the butt.

"You lost?" someone said behind me.

Startled, I spun around.

It was the black woman who stood there smiling. "Tall and good reflexes," she said.

"Uh, no," I stammered. "I mean, yeah. I guess so. I didn't know there was a boxing ring here."

"Yep," the woman said. "This is my boxing ring. I train the toughest girls in the Rockies."

The woman crossed her arms over her chest. She looked me up and down. "You like what you saw in there?"

I didn't even bother to pretend. "Yeah. I mean, I didn't know women could box."

The two women got up from their crunches and toweled off. When they turned toward the glass I could see that they weren't much older than me.

"You train girls *my* age to box?"

She laughed. "Best age to train them. Teenage girls got lots of anger they need to get out. They're just itchin' to hit something or some*body*."

She stuck her hand out. "Name's Kitty. Kitty Olsen."

Her grip was like a vise. "I'm Mardie," I managed to squeak. "Mardie Wolfe."

24

"Proud to meet you, Mardie Wolfe. Come on back and let me show you around."

On the drive home, I smiled into the dark, tapping my foot like a maniac. I loved the smell of sweat and leather in the training room. I loved the sound of the small hanging bag going *bip*-bip-bip, *bip*-bip-bip, and the dry slap of the jump rope against the floor.

Mirrors and movie posters from *Girl Fight* and *Million Dollar Baby* had ringed the room.

But most of all, though, I couldn't stop thinking about how strong and focused those girls looked, boxing up there in the ring. Dancing around each other with those big gloves on, jabbing at each other's heads and arms, they looked like they didn't give a shit what anybody else thought.

Amy's voice interrupted my thoughts. "Looks like you're about to bust. What are you so excited about, Mardie?"

I glanced over at her. "Did you know there's a boxing ring at the gym?"

"Sure I do," she said. "I thought about taking lessons, but I went with Tai Chi instead."

"There were girl boxers in there," I said.

"Yep," Amy said. "They have classes for both guys and girls."

We pulled into the garage. Amy turned off the car, pressing the remote to close the garage door.

"I think boxing would be so cool," I said.

"Maybe you could sign up for lessons," she said. "I

take Tai Chi Tuesday nights, too, when there's boxing, and I want to try the spinning class on Thursday nights. We can talk to your dad. I can't promise he'll say yes, but if you ask him nice, he'll be more inclined. You catch more flies with honey than with vinegar."

Oh, yeah. Right.

Here's how it went the next night at dinner:

Dad: "*Boxing* lessons? Why do you want to take *boxing* lessons?"

Me: "I don't know, Dad. I just do."

Dad: "I don't think so, bug. Boxing's much too violent. I've never understood why anybody'd want to do that to themselves. Besides, I'm not about to let some guy hit my daughter."

Amy: "Dave, the men and women train on different nights. They never box each other."

Me: "You'd let Michael do it, if he was the one who wanted to box."

Dad: "That's different, Mardie."

Me: "Different how? Because he's a guy?"

Dad: "Well, yes. Look, I'm glad you want to do something besides sit around and watch TV. Why don't you join the girls soccer team at school? You used to love playing soccer."

Me (trying really hard to be nice): "I've done soccer, Dad. Now I want to try boxing."

Dad: "What about lacrosse, then? I think they just started a girls lacrosse team at the high school, didn't they, Michael?"

Michael shrugged.

Me: "I'm not Michael. I don't *want* to play lacrosse."

I took a deep breath. "Let me just try it, Dad. You're always saying I need to develop new interests. Now's my chance."

Amy: "Never hurts these days for a female to know how to defend herself, honey. I almost took lessons myself."

Dad (tapping his fork): "You really want to try this, bug?"

I nodded.

Dad: "All right. Guess I'm outnumbered. You can try it, Mardie. But you have to get your grades up if you want to keep going."

Yes! I gave Dad a quick hug and took our plates to the kitchen. Boxing was going to be so cool.

THREE

"You came back!" Kitty said as I dumped my towel and water bottle on a chair. "We worked you pretty hard last time. Were you sore the next day?"

"A little, maybe," I said.

Sore couldn't begin to describe how I felt after those first few lessons. Every part of me hurt: my legs, stomach, shoulders, hands, even my toes.

Kitty clapped her hands. "Okay, ladies, grab a mat. Let's get started. Everyone on your back for crunches until I call time. Then flip over and do the same for pushups."

I really hated pushups.

Next came leg lunges, up and down the long hallway, then five minutes of jumping rope. The first night I went to this class, I nearly killed myself jumping rope. The other girls made it look like it was nothing. But I was way out of practice.

After everyone finished, Kitty divided the class into groups. Some worked the heavy bag, some shadowboxed in front of mirrors. Others took turns working the speed bag hanging in the doorway. Kitty called time after five minutes, then you moved on to the next form of torture.

The lucky ones went down to the ring. "Wrap your hands and get busy, ladies," Kitty called to them.

She waved me over to a bench, then pulled a roll of bright purple athletic gauze from her gym bag. "Right hand out. Spread your fingers." Kitty wound the gauze over my palm, then across the back of my hand and up to my wrist. She did this over and over, until a thick pad protected my knuckles. "Make a fist," she said. "Too tight?"

I shook my head no.

"Now the left one," she said.

There was something soothing about having Kitty wrap my hands. I was actually kind of disappointed when she said, "Okay, Miss Mardie. Thursday night I'll teach you how to do this yourself. Every fighter needs to know how to wrap their own hands." She stood up. "Tonight let's start you out on the heavy bag."

Kitty took me over to one of the big leather bags hanging on a chain from the ceiling.

"You've got to treat that bag like a guy you want to beat the crap out of," Kitty said. "But you got to be smart about it. Stalk it, move *with* it."

I slammed my fist as hard as I could into the center of the bag. Pain shot through my hand all the way up to my shoulder.

"Whoa, girl," Kitty said, stopping the bag's sway. "You've got a heck of a punch. But you got to use your brain, too. As the master said a long time ago, 'It is always

29

best to permit the enemy to defeat himself with little effort on your part.' "

She took off her sweatshirt jacket and stepped up to the bag. "Observe." Then, knees bent and chin tucked, Kitty wove forward and back, shifting her weight lightly on the balls of her feet.

"You throw your punch when the bag moves *away* from you, like this. Otherwise, the bag has the momentum." Her black, wiry arm shot out quick as a snake, turning from her waist as she punched.

She stepped back and gave the bag a push. "Okay. Now try it again. Do it the way I just showed you."

I threw a punch, knowing it was all wrong. "I can't. It's instinct to hit out when the bag is coming at me. The other way doesn't seem natural."

Kitty laughed. "Nothing in boxing is 'natural,' girl-friend, except protecting yourself when someone's trying to beat the crap out of you."

I took a deep breath and tried again.

"Better," Kitty said. "Remember to move your feet, and focus on the bag. And snap that little white butt of yours into your punch."

Next rotation brought me to the speed bag, and I was hideous at it. I knew from watching Kitty and the other girls that it was all in the rhythm. But this white girl had no rhythm so far.

I slapped at the bag in frustration. "Piece of crap."

Kitty called out, "Destiny, go help Mardie on the speed bag."

I'd noticed Destiny the first night I came to class. Who

wouldn't notice her? She was built like a tank. Her long black hair had these cool bright blue streaks, and she had stars tattooed across her brown chest. All the other girls laughed and joked around; not Destiny. I'd never even seen her smile.

She intimidated the hell out of me.

Destiny stepped up to the speed bag. "Watch me," she said. Her wrapped hands moved quickly and effortlessly. She stopped, then said, "Now, you."

I felt like a total spaz trying to work the bag like she did. Then I dropped my exhausted arms. "I can't do it. I feel totally stupid."

Destiny nodded. "You look pretty stupid, too, but you'll get better—if you want to." Stepping back to the evil bag, she went on, "Let me show you a couple of things. First off, the point of boxing is not to hit hard, it's to hit *right*, okay?"

I shrugged.

"The problem is you're hitting the bag with your knuckles."

"Well, what am I supposed to hit it with? My elbow?"

She ignored my sarcasm. "No, a knife."

"Excuse me?"

"Give me your hand," Destiny said.

I inched out my left hand.

"Now pretend you're holding a knife."

I curled my fingers around an imaginary handle.

"Good. Now pretend you're stabbing the bag rather than punching it."

This time, I batted at the bag with the meaty butt of my hand.

31

"Okay, now watch my feet and hips."

Destiny rocked back and forth, foot to foot, her hips turning. "Your power is always in your center," she said.

Then Kitty appeared at my elbow. "How's it going, ladies?"

Destiny shrugged. "She'll get it if she wants."

"It's really hard, though," I replied.

"It's rhythm and hand-eye coordination," Kitty said. "But like most of life, it's also all about balance. Let's see you work the bag."

I sighed, stepped forward, and raised my fists. Focusing on the small bag and an imaginary knife, I punched.

"Don't forget your feet and hips," Kitty said.

But as soon as I tried to think about shifting my weight and turning my hips like Destiny, I lost what little rhythm I had.

"Focus, Mardie," Kitty said. "You're not focused."

"I'll never get this right," I complained. "It's not fair to expect somebody to be able to do this right away."

Kitty clamped a hand on my shoulder and pointed to a sign above the doorway to the locker room.

"Mardie, can you read?"

"Of course."

"Then read that big sign over there. Out loud."

The room went suddenly quiet. Then I read the bright red words:

ARGUE FOR YOUR LIMITATIONS
AND SURE ENOUGH, THEY'RE YOURS

I was the only one in the locker room when I looked around. I stared at the poster of a gorgeous, buff black woman. Her fists were raised. Her eyes bored into mine like lasers. "What did I get my lame ass into?" I asked her.

I heard the door open and swish closed. "Don't worry. We've all had to read that sign out loud at some point or another."

I looked up. The Latina girl from my school grinned.

I jerked a sweatshirt over my head. "It doesn't make any sense."

She laughed. "It will if you stick it out. Name's Shireen, by the way. I've seen you at school."

I jerked my thumb at a big hand-lettered sign above the sinks. "Like that sign, too? It doesn't make a hell of a lot of sense either."

The big black letters read:

KITTY'S RULES:

*NO CUSSIN'

*NO WHININ'

*NO FIGHTIN'

"I mean, hello. Aren't we here to fight?"

Shireen ran her fingers through her short black hair. She twisted the ends into little spikes. "No, not to fight," she said. "To *box*."

I zipped up my jacket. "I just want to get in the ring and *fight*," I said. "The hell with this other stuff."

Shireen looked me up and down. Snapping her gum, she shot back, "Two things you better learn real fast, *chica*, if you're going to be a boxer: patience and no whining. As nice as she is, Kitty won't stand for whiners."

"And," she said, slamming her locker shut, "you go in the ring when Kitty says you're *ready*. Trust me, everything you do in the gym leads you one step closer to the ring."

"So how's the boxing going?" Dad asked when we got home. "Is it what you thought it would be?"

I shrugged. "I guess. It's kind of harder than I thought."

"Everything new is hard at first. Remember how hard soccer was when you first started?"

But I didn't really. It seemed like I always knew how to play.

"You're lucky," Dad said. "Unlike your old man, you're a natural athlete. It'll get easier fast."

But it wasn't fast enough for me.

I jumped rope. I ground out crunches and pushups (which actually got easier over the next couple of weeks). I worked the heavy bag and the speed bag. Threw jabs and combos at myself in the mirrors. And I did begin to get better. But that didn't matter because I wasn't in the ring. All the others—Suze, Shireen, Chris, and, of course, Destiny at least got to spar.

Envy gnawed at my stomach. And as usual, when we got in the car Amy started chattering away. She has this incredibly annoying habit of picking up a conversation you had two days ago, like you just left off two minutes ago. I wanted to scream at her to just shut up, and I had no idea what the hell she was talking about.

At the stoplight she pointed across the street. "Isn't that your friend from boxing?"

I looked at the person standing under the streetlight, and sure enough it was Shireen, waiting at the bus stop. "I wouldn't say we're actually friends," I said. Shireen was annoying, too, the way she joked and played around all the time.

Amy did a U-turn in the middle of the street. "Let's give her a ride," she said. "No sense in her waiting for a bus when we can take her instead."

I groaned. "Amy, can't we just go home?"

Amy waved Shireen inside the van. "We'll give you a ride," she said.

Shireen flashed me a grin. "Thanks a lot!" she said, settling into the backseat.

"I thought your mom usually picks you up," I commented. There must have been something in my voice because Amy shot me one of her looks.

Shireen was oblivious. "Not on Thursday nights. She has class on Monday and Thursday nights, so I have to take the bus."

"Oh? What kind of class is she taking?" Amy asked.

"She's studying to become a CPA," Shireen said.

"Wow," Amy said. "That's great. She must like numbers."

"Yeah," Shireen said. "She's really smart. She's an accountant at Summit Memorial Hospital, been there the last few years. She likes it and all, but she wants to start her own business."

"What does your father do?" Amy asked.

Shireen actually paused for a long second, enough so that Amy glanced at her in the rearview mirror.

"My dad's in the reserves," she replied. "He was deployed six months ago. For the second time."

"Oh gosh," Amy said. "That must be hard."

I turned in my seat and looked at Shireen. For the first time since I'd known her, she actually wasn't smiling.

"Yeah," she said, studying the seat belt buckle. "We miss him a whole lot."

Amy and I glanced at each other; for once she was at a loss for words.

"Oh hey," Shireen said. "There's my place. Almost let you pass it! Then you'd be stuck with me and . . ." Her mouth was off and running again, back to the same old Shireen.

Amy pulled into the driveway of the low brick duplex. Bikes and abandoned toys littered the walkway.

Shireen jumped out of the van and slung her duffle bag over her shoulder. Poking her head back inside the car, she said, "Thanks again for the ride. I know it was out of your way and all." Then the porch light came on and the front door opened.

"No problem," Amy said. "Anytime."

Shireen grinned at me. "You looked good on the speed bag tonight, *chica*. See you there on Tuesday."

FOUR

I was late again for English.

"Glad you could join us, Mardie," Mr. Edison said.

"Sorry," I mumbled, slipping into my seat. The word of the day was scrawled across the board. I leaned down to get my dictionary out of my pack. Megan, who sat right next to me, slipped me a piece of paper. I unfolded the note. "Skip 6th. Meet me behind the P.O." I was already behind in my sixth-period pre-calculus class. If I wasn't careful, I'd flunk.

I looked across at Megan. She raised one pierced eyebrow and grinned like I was her new best friend. Who knows? Maybe I was.

Megan is one of those girls your parents don't want you to hang with. She smokes, she drinks, and she's supposedly hooked up with half the guys in the high school. Of course, since she's looked about eighteen ever since middle school, the same thing was said about her even then. Not that she cares what anyone says about her. She'd just wink and tell them to kiss her sweet behind. I've always liked that about her.

The hill behind the post office was covered with low

sagebrush and scrub oaks, and the occasional patch of cactus, with a solitary pinion pine at the top of the hill.

Megan and I sat on a bench made out of sandstone slabs. Megan inhaled deeply, then passed me the joint. In a cloud of exhaled smoke she said, "So you and Ben Richter, huh?"

I shrugged, not wanting to waste the hit I'd taken.

"Ben's hot, no doubt," Megan continued. "Of course, he's worked his way through most of the female population in South Eden."

I looked at the sun shining through Megan's magenta hair. "Meaning what?" I asked.

With a short laugh, Megan replied, "Meaning if you're doing it with him, you better be using a rubber."

My face burned. "We're not doing anything like that," I said.

"Well, you better get a move on, girlfriend," she said, flicking the butt of the joint into the sage. "That's why he dumped Celeste, that little princess. She wasn't giving him any."

I picked at the mud on the bottom of my jeans, not wanting to look at Megan. She doesn't know I'm still a virgin. The idea of sex is kind of exciting, but it's also a little scary. And so far, scary is winning.

Megan stood up and stretched, her tight shirt sliding up. A tattooed rose curled around her belly button. "I mean, you're good looking and all. And lots of guys'd like to hook up with you. But looks only keep someone like Ben Richter interested for so long."

My heart sank hearing her say this.

Back in town, Megan said, "I need some things from the drugstore."

I followed her into the warmth of the too bright store. Even though Thanksgiving hadn't even come yet, Christmas stuff was everywhere: Christmas cards, cheap red-and-white stockings, bags of brightly colored bows. It made me sick to see it. Why did they always rush things like that? It took the fun out of the holidays when they finally arrived. Couldn't we enjoy our holidays one at a time?

Megan slipped a tube of lipstick into her coat pocket. She looked at me over her shoulder and winked. Next into her pocket went some eyeliner, then a box of fake nails and some nail polish. "We should get you some rubbers," she laughed, grabbing a spiral notebook and a box of pens.

She strolled toward the checkout. "The secret is to always buy something. Otherwise they get suspicious when girls wander in but don't buy anything," she said under her breath.

My heart pounded, my hands clammy. Sure, I'd swiped the occasional candy bar or eyeliner, but never this much stuff. What if we got caught?

Megan just smiled, flirting with the guy at the register like they were long lost lovers.

Back outside the drugstore, I finally felt like I could breathe again. My heart slid from my throat back down to my chest, and I tingled all over, alive.

Megan laughed as she took out a pack of cigarettes. "I hope you were taking notes, little Mardie. That guy probably had a boner behind the counter."

Megan offered me a cigarette. I was just about to take

it when I saw my brother Michael walking across the parking lot toward us. *Shit.*

He nodded in that superior way he has. "Afternoon, ladies."

Megan eyed him and smirked. "Hey, big guy. I don't think we've ever had the pleasure of meeting before."

Michael pointedly ignored her.

"Of course," Megan said in this super snarky way, "I'm not exactly your *type*, am I?"

"Mom's looking for you, Mar," he said. "But you might want to get some Visine before you go home. Your eyes are so red, you could stop traffic."

Megan laughed and pulled a little white bottle from her bottomless coat pocket. "I'm way ahead of you."

Michael shook his head and sighed. "Whatever. Just go home, Mardie, before you get into even more trouble."

"That brother of yours is hot," Megan said at the bus stop.

I looked down the street for the bus.

"That hair, those eyes," Megan said dramatically. "Too bad he's gay."

I did a double take. "What?"

"Your brother," Megan said as if she were talking to an idiot. "He's gay."

The earth shifted under my feet, everything off kilter. "You're crazy, Megan. He's not gay!"

Megan dropped her cigarette on the sidewalk as her bus sighed to a stop. "Give me a friggin' break, Mardie," she said as she climbed up the bus steps. "Everybody knows about it."

I stood there staring after the bus as it slipped into traffic. *Michael gay?* I'd known him all my life. It couldn't be true, could it?

Later that week, we woke to the first snowfall of the season.

"Never fails," Amy said. "Just when it's time for the little kids to dress up in their Halloween costumes, we get a huge snowstorm and it turns cold. Poor kids have the choice of wearing big ol' coats over their costumes or freezing their little behinds off."

She handed Michael the last of the groceries to put away. "What are y'all planning for Halloween?" she asked.

"Gotta work," Michael said.

"What about you, Mardie?" Amy asked.

I grabbed a soda from the fridge. "Not much, since I'm grounded. Guess I'll just go to the gym and work out."

"Let me talk to your dad. You've been pretty good. Maybe we can grant you an early reprieve."

That night, as I sat at my desk trying to get caught up on my pre-calc homework, Dad stuck his head in the door.

"You doing homework, bug?"

"No, I'm writing the story of my life: *Autobiography of a Loser.*"

He sighed.

I shrugged. "Pre-calc. My favorite."

Dad made a face. "I hate math. I wouldn't be any help to you there. But Michael could help you if you need it."

I'd made a point of avoiding Michael ever since Megan's revelation. It was just too weird to even think about.

"Anyway," Dad said. "If you want to go do something for Halloween, that's okay with me. You've been pretty good lately, so go ahead. Heck, we'll even give you your cell phone back."

"Thanks, Dad."

He looked up at the ceiling. "About time to put some new stars and planets up, isn't it?" he asked.

"Sure, Dad."

I had a hard time concentrating at training Thursday night. Just that afternoon while I was getting stuff out of my locker, Ben had come up behind me and slipped an arm around my waist.

"You coming to Rick's Halloween party Saturday night?"

I smiled up at him. "I could. The 'rents un-grounded me early, since I've been such a good girl and all."

Ben's grin widened. My knees turned to water. "Oh, but I like it a lot better when you're a bad, bad girl," Ben said.

Now all I could think about was going to the party with Ben, what I would wear, and how hideously huge my butt felt.

"Watch your footwork, Mardie," Kitty reminded me for the millionth time. "You've got the attention span of a gnat tonight."

Later when I took just a short little break, she commented, "You're dragging butt tonight, girl."

"I'm just tired, Kitty."

She looked at me with narrowed eyes. "Did you eat good food like I told you? Are you getting plenty of rest?"

Actually, I hadn't eaten much the last couple of days. The jeans I planned to wear Friday night were feeling a bit too snug and I wanted to do something about it.

"You're too thin, Mardie. You'll never make it as a boxer if you don't put some weight on and treat your body with respect."

I got up and shadowboxed in front of the mirror. I threw a quick right at my reflection. *No way am I going to look all big and beefy like Destiny*. I hooked a jab with my left. *And that Shireen with her big Latino butt, no way.*

I gathered up my stuff and headed out to meet Amy.

"So you coming Saturday night?" Kitty asked. "Most of the other girls are. We could work out in costumes!"

"Sorry," I said, not looking at her. "I have other plans."

"Yes, Dad," I said. "For the millionth time, Rick's parents will be at the party."

It was Saturday night. I was meeting Ben at the Shop-N-Go in forty minutes. The last thing I wanted to be doing was setting the table and eating.

"What's the number over there?" Amy asked from the kitchen.

"I don't know. I've never called him," I said.

"I'd like to talk to his folks," Amy said. She took the lasagna out of the oven. It smelled awesome. "Just to make sure."

I thumped the plates on the dining room table, mumbling, "It's just *so comforting* when your parents trust you."

Amy turned around, green eyes flashing.

Dad cut her off. "We have to trust her sometime, honey. She hasn't given us any reason not to lately." Dad put an arm around me. "We can trust you, right, bug?"

Without looking at him, I said, "Sure."

Amy said nothing, but her pale face flushed. She jerked opened the refrigerator, her shoulders tense.

"And who is this, giving you a ride to the party?" Dad asked.

"Um, Megan's dad is taking us," I lied.

"And bringing you home, too?"

"Yeah, sure," I said.

The party was cranking when Ben and I got there. Someone slapped Ben on the back and handed him a beer. Alexis laughed with Sam over in the corner. Megan slinked past in an impossibly low-cut shirt. Another girl I recognized from history class was draped all over Eric Lindstrom, the King of the Jock Table.

"Looks like Eric is going to score big time tonight," Ben said, raising his beer in Eric's direction.

"How do you know him?" I asked.

"Eric's dad works with my dad at his car dealership. Eric and I have been hanging out ever since second grade."

The guy who'd given Ben the beer when we first arrived brought him another one. "How's it going, Ben? Introduce me to your date," he said, smiling.

Ben slipped an arm around my waist. "This is Mardie Wolfe, and tonight she's all mine."

"Very glad to meet you, Mardie. I'm Rick. Actually, we're both in Mr. Edison's English class. You probably haven't noticed me, though."

I had some vague memory of him over by the window in class, but truthfully, he wasn't someone who exactly stood out for any reason. Average height, average hair, average looks.

Covering up my embarrassment, I said, "I thought your parents were going to be here."

Rick laughed. "Are you kidding? Wouldn't be much of a party if they were. They're at some friend's party over in Snyderville. If I know my dad, he'll drink so much they'll have to spend the night." I was glad I hadn't known Rick's phone number.

Grabbing a fistful of pretzels, Rick said, "Is your brother Michael Wolfe?"

"Yeah," I said.

"He's smart. He's tutored me at the math lab a couple of times. Good lacrosse player, too."

"Did you say Wolfe?" a voice said behind me. Eric and the blond leech attached to his side strolled up.

"Yeah," Rick said. "Michael Wolfe. This is his sister."

Eric got a sour look on his face. "He's a queer."

Ben started to laugh.

I shot him a look. "He is *not* queer."

"Oh right," Ben said. "He's head of the Chess Club.

Everyone knows the guys in the Chess Club are a bunch of fags."

"He's also the captain of the lacrosse team," I said.

"That's because we don't let queers on the football team," Eric sneered.

I clenched my fists. I got right in Eric's face and spat back, "He's too smart to play football."

Ben threw back his head and laughed. "She's got you there, dude!" Eric's ice blue eyes went hard.

Rick put his hands up. "Come on, guys. Lighten up."

Eric took one step closer, the toes of his shoes actually touching mine.

I didn't even blink.

Finally, Ben put his hand on Eric's shoulder. "Let's step outside, bro. I got some good weed I want you to try."

I was not invited. I watched them disappear through the patio doors.

"Hey, how's it going?" Alexis said, handing me a beer.

"Okay, I guess."

"What do you mean, just okay? Geez, Mardie, you're with Ben Richter. You're the envy of every girl here."

My heart was still pounding. I wanted to punch Eric Lindstrom.

"Anyway," she said. "I'm glad you're off restriction. I was thinking I'd have to take up knitting or reading to the blind, I was so bored with you grounded. I guess you'll stop going to the gym so much now."

I took a deep breath and tried to relax. "I don't know. Maybe."

I turned my back on the patio. "So how's Sam doing?

Are his parents still talking about sending him to that Nazi school?"

Alexis laughed. "Well, they think he's going to these 'Just Say No' classes two times a week."

"But he's not?" I asked.

"He's coming to my house. My mom's taking a computer class in the afternoons."

"Convenient," I said

"Yeah," Alexis said, glancing across the room at Sam. "Sometimes I think maybe too convenient."

"What do you—"

Ben came up behind me and whispered in my ear, "Miss me?"

I smiled up at him. "Missed you, but not that asshole, Eric."

Alexis winked and headed back to Sam.

"Now, Miss Wolfe," Ben said, "would you care to join me for a tour of the house?"

The first bedroom was obviously Rick's little sister's room. I did not want to make out with a bunch of dolls and stuffed animals watching.

When Ben flipped on the light in the second bedroom, Megan and some guy were seriously lip locked on the bed. "Shit! Turn the light off and get out of here!"

"Sorry," I stammered. I turned my face away so Ben couldn't see how embarrassed I was.

Ben led me upstairs and opened another bedroom door. "Looks like three's the charm," he said.

He didn't bother turning on the light. He ran his hand through my hair, lifted it in one large hand, then let it fall back to my waist. "Amazing," he said.

He pulled me to him, moving toward the bed as he kissed my neck. "Now, where were we?"

I don't know if it was the beer or the strangeness of being in a dark bedroom with a guy. Whatever it was, I felt totally outside of myself. It was like I was watching Ben's hands on someone else's body.

He moved on top of me, kissing my neck and shoulders. Part of me wanted to be with him, be absorbed by him as completely as possible. Another part of me just wanted to be back in my own bed, in my own room.

Ben didn't even notice I wasn't really there.

"God, Mardie," Ben groaned, grinding himself into my pelvis. I wasn't sure what I was supposed to do.

Suddenly I didn't want to be there. I tried to work my way out from under him. He lifted his head from the nook of my shoulder. "Just relax, Mardie," he mumbled. And then he passed out.

I slipped out of the bedroom. I looked everywhere for Alexis and Sam, but they were MIA. *Crap, crap, crap.*

I stood outside on Rick's patio. My cell phone shook in my cold hand. I dialed Michael's number.

"This is Michael."

For a second I was confused by this deep voice that belonged to my brother.

"Hello?"

"Yeah, Michael. It's me. What time do you get off tonight?" Michael's job at the radio station had weird hours, especially on the weekends.

"Why?" he asked suspiciously.

"I need a ride home from this party. And please don't ask why."

"Christ, Mardie. When are you going to grow up?"

I tried like hell to keep the frustration out of my voice. "Just do it, Michael. Please. The last thing I need from you is a lecture."

That old Volkswagen never did get warm, no matter how long you drove it. "But it gets me where I want to go," Michael always said. "That's what counts."

I huddled deeper in my thin shirt, sitting on my hands to keep them warm.

"So how're you going to explain this one to Dad and Mom?"

"I'll think of something," I said. "Besides, she's not our real mom."

Michael looked over at me. "What's with you, Mardie? Why do you all of a sudden have this thing about Amy?"

I propped one foot up on the dashboard and looked out at the night sky.

"Amy's the closest thing we've had to a real mother for the last ten years," Michael said.

I watched one star that appeared brighter than the others. "Do you ever wonder what our life would be like if Mom hadn't died?" I asked.

Michael turned down the street to our house. "No, Mardie, I can honestly say I haven't."

We pulled into the drive. Michael cut the engine and turned off the lights.

"Look, Mardie, I don't know what kind of adolescent-girl crisis you're going through, but we have it pretty good. When we were little, Amy came to all my stupid band concerts and all your soccer games. She helped us with our homework, and took you horseback riding all the time. I think she's cool to talk with."

I snorted, "Right, books and foreign films. That's all you guys ever talk about. It's boring." *And gay.*

"And," Michael continued, ignoring me. "Dad's a good guy. He sewed our Halloween costumes every year—"

"That's because he's cheap," I interrupted.

"He's done the best he can, Mardie. They may not be perfect, but they've always let us be who we are."

I'd had more than enough of Saint Michael's holier-than-thou crap. Opening the car door, I said, "Oh really, Michael? Is that why you've never told them you're gay?"

In the washed-out light of the car interior, his face turned white, his mouth dropped open. For once, I had the last word.

FIVE

Tuesday night at the gym, the same thing I'd been doing for the last six weeks: crunches, pushups, "Time!" Lunges, jumping rope, "Time!" Heavy bag, speed bag, shadowboxing, "Time!"

Shadowboxing in front of the big mirrors, all I could focus on was how hideously huge my butt was and the latest zit blooming on my forehead. But as I watched the other girls—Shireen, Suze, Chris, Destiny—shadowboxing, I noticed something. They weren't worried about how they looked, or at least how they might look in the eyes of some guy. They focused on being strong, fast, and balanced.

I took a deep breath and tried to do the same. Feet shoulder-width apart, knees bent, chin tucked. Push all the way through that left.

"Looking good tonight, Mardie," Kitty said. "Things are coming together for you. You feel good?"

"Yeah," I said, pushing my hair out of my face. "I feel pretty good."

"Then I think it's time we got you in the ring."

Yes!

I slipped my hands into the huge leather gloves. They still felt warm and just a little damp from the last person who wore them.

As Kitty laced them up she said, "Okay. When I say one, it's a straight right. When I say two, you hook left. Three is jab and four is uppercut. Got it?"

Destiny strapped the training mitts on Kitty's hands. They looked like padded Ping-Pong paddles. We ducked under the ropes.

I stood in the middle of the ring. The bright overhead lights blocked out everything outside of the ring. We were in our own little universe.

Kitty held up her hands. "Feet shoulder-width apart, knees bent. Ready?"

I nodded and flexed my knees.

"One! Three! Two! Four!" she barked. "Turn your waist, Mardie! Move your feet! Keep your hands up! Hands up! Focus! Focus!"

After just three minutes, my arms and brain were exhausted. Who knew boxing could wear your brain out, too? Still, it felt sweet to be up there in the ring, just me and Kitty.

"You look good up there, Mardie." Amy leaned against the doorjamb, smiling.

She walked over to the side of the ring, hand extended. "I'm Amy Bayne, Mardie's stepmother."

Kitty pulled off the training mitts and grasped Amy's hand.

"Kitty Olsen. Proud to meet you. Your girl here's got a lot of natural talent."

Amy smiled up at me. "Yeah? Doesn't surprise me, really. She's always been athletic. Played soccer for years, practically lived on the back of a horse. Darned good basketball player for a while, too, but she didn't stick with it."

"Well," Kitty said. "I hope she sticks with this. She's progressed more in six weeks than some do in six months. She could go places with her talent."

I didn't know whether to crawl in a hole or burst with pride.

"It's her choice," Amy said.

On the drive home, Amy chatted away while I thought about being in the ring. I was tired, but I still felt an electric buzz in my arms and legs. I hadn't felt this excited about anything since—

"Earth to Mardie," Amy said.

I blinked back to the inside of the car. "What?"

"I just asked if you ever see Chelsea and Nicole."

I blinked again. I had no idea what she was talking about.

"I saw Chelsea's mother at the grocery store yesterday," Amy said. "And it reminded me how long it's been since I've seen Chelsea. And how she and Nicole used to hang out at the house with you and Alexis all the time. 'The Gang of Four' your dad and I used to call y'all."

I shrugged. "That was a long time ago."

Amy laughed. "Just two or three years. Not that long."

Maybe not to her, but to me it felt like a million years.

We'd all been close. We went to the same elementary schools, played on the same soccer teams, went to the same birthday parties.

Eighth grade, though, things started to change. All of a sudden, Chelsea became obsessed with fashion and labels. No way would she associate with an anti-fashion geek like me. And Nicole's passion for gymnastics morphed into cheerleading in ninth grade. Now she's Queen Bee of the Cheerleader Table in the cafeteria. They both have an amazing ability to look right through me.

"They're into other things now," I said and changed the subject.

Friday night, Dad fixed a big pot of chili and a skillet of cornbread. I was too nervous to eat. Ben and I were going to the football game. Dad and Amy insisted Ben pick me up at the house so they could meet him.

If Ben'd been smoking or drinking, I was sunk. Dad probably wouldn't pick up on it, but Amy would. She doesn't miss things like that.

The doorbell rang. Ben looked especially handsome but smelled like pot. It was like, couldn't he have waited until *after* he met my parents?

He stepped into the foyer and shook snow from his hair. He smiled like he'd won the lottery. Max growled, circling his legs.

"Amy," I called as I pulled on my coat. "Call Max."

Amy acted like she was too engrossed in the football game on TV to hear me, but I knew she could.

Ben bent down to pat Max's head. Max growled and moved away.

"Well, we better get going," I said.

"Not so fast, Mardie," Dad said. "We'd like to meet your friend." My dad was in an apron that said KISS THE COOK.

Before I could protest, Ben stepped into the living room.

"Glad to meet you, Mr. Wolfe," he said, extending his hand. "I'm Ben Richter. I'm a big fan of your daughter here."

Please don't let him smell the pot, I prayed.

Dad smiled and took off the lobster-shaped oven mitts. "That makes two of us."

"Okay," I said, tugging on his sleeve. "You've met Dad. Now let's go."

Ben turned to me. "What's your big hurry, Mardie? I haven't met your mom yet."

"Stepmom," I said quickly.

He sauntered across to the living room, smile now amped up another hundred watts.

"Whatever," he said. "I'm glad to meet you, Mrs. Wolfe."

I knew what was coming next.

Amy unfolded herself from the couch, drew herself up to her full height, and extended her hand. "Glad to meet you, Ben. And my name is Amy *Bayne*, not Wolfe."

Ben took her hand. Max growled and Amy sniffed. Crap.

"Cool. But don't I detect a Southern accent?"

"Yes," Amy said. "I was born and raised in Georgia."

"Well then," Ben grinned. "I guess that makes you a Georgia peach."

Amy studied him like a cat trying to decide whether to kill her prey or toy with it a little longer. She looked at me, then said, "I doubt Mardie would agree with that."

Just as Amy was about to move in for the kill, Michael padded downstairs.

He nodded at Ben. "How's it going, Richter?"

Ben's high-watt grin dimmed. His eyes hardened. "Not bad, Wolfe. Not bad at all. How's the Chess Club?"

Michael didn't answer.

Dad said, "Oh, you play chess, Ben? Mardie's a great chess player, but not as good as her brother. Still, watch her. She's got a killer instinct."

I'd had enough. "We're going to be late if we don't go now, Ben."

The smile switched on again. "Great to meet you, Mr. Wolfe. I'll look after Mardie for you."

"I'll hold you to that, Ben. And call me Dave." Dad was charmed.

Ben turned to Amy and Michael. Michael was busy scratching behind Max's ear, pointedly ignoring Ben. "It was great to meet you, too, Mrs., uh, Bayne. Can I call you Amy?"

With a level look, she said, "Mrs. Bayne is just fine."

Okay, we didn't exactly go to the game. We huddled in the back of Sam's car parked behind the stadium, the glowing tip of the joint moving through the darkness like a firefly.

THE RING

The first time I saw fireflies, I was seven. We'd gone to Georgia to visit Amy's sister, Lynn. Lynn and her best friend, Jan, live way out in the country in the hills of north Georgia.

At night we'd sit on the front porch, listening to the voices of bullfrogs and insects. And then, by some magical agreement between fading light and insect, the fireflies would appear. They floated out, one by one. Before you knew it, the night was filled with them.

Ben kissed the side of my mouth, startling me.

"You were a million miles away," he said. "With that dreamy look on your face, I'm guessing you were thinking about me."

I smiled. "You bet."

The house was dark when Ben pulled up in our driveway. He pulled me close, kissing me hard. His hand wormed its way underneath my coat, trying to untuck my shirt. His hand found my bare belly.

I jerked away. "Your hand is freezing," I said.

"I know," he said. "I need a nice place to warm it up. Any suggestions?"

Just then, headlights swung in behind, putting us in a spotlight. "Jesus Christ!" Ben said, pulling his hand out from my shirt.

"It's Michael," I said. "He must be coming home from work."

"Or a hot date," Ben said.

The car door slammed. Michael's footsteps crunched in the snow. "I better get inside," I said, sliding across the car seat.

Ben's eyes followed Michael.

I touched Ben's sleeve. "See you soon?"

"Yeah sure," he said, starting up his car. "I'll call you."

Michael was wandering around the living room brushing his teeth when I came in. He said he always did his best thinking when he brushed his teeth.

Have I mentioned Michael's weird?

He spit his toothpaste in the kitchen sink. "So why are you spending so much time with that loser?"

"You shouldn't talk about yourself that way, dear brother."

"You know who I mean, smart ass. Richter has a reputation."

"As what?" I asked, picking at some leftover cornbread.

"As a redneck, for one thing," Michael said.

"I wouldn't talk too much about reputations, Michael."

Michael's face flushed. "Come on, Mardie," he said. "You're way better than that Neanderthal, Ben, and that skank, Megan. You don't need them. Why do you care what they think?"

All of a sudden, I felt tired. How could I explain to someone like Michael why it mattered, when I couldn't even explain it to myself?

"Thanks," I said. "But it's hard to take you seriously when you've got toothpaste drooling out of your mouth. You look like a rabid dog."

Tuesday night at boxing, I must have been in what they call "the zone." Everything seemed to come together. Yes, this white girl even got her rhythm going.

I worked the speed bag effortlessly. Some of the other girls stopped to watch me work the heavy bag.

I threw killer combinations at my image in the mirror. Kitty said some of the most famous boxers in the world have been lefties like me.

"You're on fire tonight, girl," Kitty said. "Let's get those big ol' gloves on and get you in the ring."

The ring. My stomach felt all fluttery whenever Kitty said that, same as when Ben kissed me.

Kitty finished wrapping my hands, then laced up the leather gloves. I didn't like how helpless they made me. I couldn't even pick my own nose or scratch an itch once they were on. But as Kitty said, there wasn't much in boxing that was natural.

I slipped through the ropes, just me and Kitty, and the lights shining bright.

Kitty barked out the combos. "One! Three! One, one, four!"

I anticipated her calls, nothing else in the world except her voice, my breathing, and the pop of leather against leather.

"Snap your waist. Good! Good footwork!" *Pop! Pop!* I felt strong, focused, and strangely free. *Pop!* I couldn't remember the last time I felt this good. *Pop! Pop!*

Then, just as I threw a hook and jab combination, I heard a familiar voice, Sam's voice, saying, "Geez, would you look at that. It's Mardie!"

I looked over my shoulder. Sam stood in the doorway, holding a basketball against one hip, grinning. And next to him was Ben.

Sam elbowed him, saying, "She could kick your ass, man!"

I dropped my hands, smiled, and shrugged. I saw myself through Ben's eyes: ugly helmet over long sweaty hair, Michael's baggy shorts and T-shirt, huge leather gloves dangling at the end of my skinny white arms. I must have looked like a clown. Or a freak. I gave an apologetic wave.

Ben shook his head in disgust, turned on his heel, and left.

Six

Three days since Ben saw me at the gym and he hadn't called.

"I knew it was too good to be true," I said to Alexis in the cafeteria. "Ben can have any girl in this school. I never knew why he bothered with me."

Alexis stirred her yogurt over and over. She seemed a million miles away. I nudged her foot under the table. She looked up, startled.

"So, did you hear anything I said?" I asked.

"Uh, something about Ben?" Alexis guessed.

I stood and grabbed my backpack. "Some friend you are."

Alexis's eyes filled with tears. "I'm sorry, Mardie. Please don't go!"

I slipped off my pack and sat down. "What's going on with you? Is it Sam?"

Alexis nodded. "Can I ask you something?"

"Sure," I said.

"Well, have you and Ben, you know . . ."

I felt my face reddening. "No, not *that*, actually."

A tear dripped off the end of Alexis's nose and landed in her raspberry yogurt. "Sam and I have," she whispered.

I felt an ugly flash of envy. "Congratulations," I said flatly. "I must be the only freaking virgin left in the entire school."

"Believe me, Mardie, it's not all it's cracked up to be."

"You're kidding, right?"

Alexis tossed her uneaten yogurt in the garbage. "It's messy, and it hurts. And the worst part is I don't know why Sam wants to hang out with me anymore."

"What do you mean?"

"I don't know, it's weird now. We were really good friends before we started doing it. I felt like I could just have fun with Sam. Kind of like I have fun with you. We could joke around and just hang out together."

"So what's the problem?" I asked.

"Now it's like all he wants to do is *that*. He doesn't want to just talk and stuff. If I don't want to have sex, he gets mad. Like I'm taking something away from him on purpose." Alexis sighed. She looked at me, her eyes red. "I want things to be the way they used to be."

Just then the bell rang for next period. "So tell Sam what you just told me," I said.

"I'll lose him if I do," Alexis said. "And then what?"

Then she'd be a nobody, like me.

That night I lay burrowed in the couch, Teddy curled up at my feet. Amy raced around getting her stuff together to go to the gym.

"Get on up, Mardie, and grab your gym bag. We need to get going."

"I don't feel that great," I said from under the afghan. "I'm not going tonight."

Amy felt my forehead. "You don't feel hot, honey. But I guess if you aren't feeling good there's no sense in going. Maybe you just need some rest."

Yeah, that's just what I needed. A rest from my miserable life.

Later, after everyone was in bed, I was wide awake. Why hadn't Ben called? Why did he have to see me up there, in that stupid ring, with those stupid gloves?

I flipped open my cell and punched in Alexis's number. Busy. I texted R U UP?

BUSY! flashed across the screen.

I texted back, NEED 2 TALK! I watched the tiny screen.

A few seconds later she texted 2 BUSY 2 TALK!

I took a deep breath, swallowed my pride, and typed in PLEASE.

I watched the screen. Five seconds. Ten seconds. No answer. Fifteen seconds. No fucking answer.

I snapped my phone closed. Alexis was never too busy to talk. We'd always talked to each other about everything. But like everything else in my life, even that was changing.

I know every freckle on Alexis's face (and how much she hates them); I know how her bottom tooth got chipped when we were in sixth grade; I went with her to buy her first bra, and I know when she got her first period. But ever since this summer, she's become more and more of a mystery to me.

I just wanted everything to stop changing.

I pulled my covers closer, a tear sliding down my cheek.

I remembered Dad teaching me to ride a bike, so scary and thrilling all at once. He held on to the back of my bike seat, running alongside, yelling, "Peddle, Mardie! Peddle!"

I'd go my wobbly way for a few minutes, then crash. Dad would help me up and get me back on the bike. "Never give up, Mardie," he'd say. "You can do it."

Off I'd go again. And again I'd hear his voice in my ear, "Peddle, Mardie! Peddle!" But this time the voice was getting farther away. I wobbled less. I looked back over my shoulder and was, for a moment, terrified to see how far away Dad was. He jumped up and down, shouting, "You're doing it, Mardie! You're doing it!" I remembered feeling proud and scared, all mixed up together. Nothing ever would be the same again.

Seven

Sam bumped my shoulder in biology lab, making me spill the beaker of foul-smelling liquid. "Crap."

"Sorry about that, Mar," Sam said, holding up his hands in mock defense. "Don't hit me! Just trying to get your attention."

"Okay, so you've got it. What do you want?"

"A bunch of us are meeting down at the quarry Friday night. Want to come?"

"I'm not sure how I'd get there," I said.

"Ben would bring you, wouldn't he?"

"How should I know," I said, remeasuring and mixing. "I haven't talked to him in over a week."

Sam shifted uncomfortably. "Huh. Well, I'll see him at basketball this afternoon. Maybe I can ask him. I'm sure he's just busy."

"Sure, thanks," I said.

Later that night, my cell phone rang. Ben's number flashed on the screen. A rush of adrenaline shot through my legs.

"Hey," I said, walking back to my bedroom, shutting the door. "It's been a while."

Ben cleared his throat. "Sorry about that. I've been busy with stuff, and time just got away from me. But, hey, I'm calling now."

I didn't say anything.

After an uncomfortable minute, Ben said, "So anyway, a bunch of us are going out to the quarry Friday night. Sam and Alexis are going. You want to go?"

I knew I shouldn't make this too easy for him. I mean, here it was the night before. It wasn't totally outside the realm of possibility that I had other plans. Even another date.

But then Ben purred into the phone, "Come on, Mardie. Come out and play."

"So anyway," Ben said to Sam as we drove out to the quarry. "This guy had the nerve to show up late for basketball tryouts. He told Coach he was late because he had to gather up the sheet music after concert choir. Can you believe that?"

"Why is that such a big deal?" Alexis asked.

Sam and Ben looked at each other and shook their heads. "First of all," Ben said, "you don't show up for tryouts late. Especially not with Coach Sloan."

"Secondly," Sam said, tossing an empty beer can over his shoulder, "the guy's queer as a two-dollar bill. He shouldn't even be trying out."

He continued, "I told Coach afterwards I don't care how tall the guy is. I'm not sharing a locker room with a queer."

I bit my lip and counted to ten. What I really wanted to do was tell them what a couple of ignorant rednecks they were. But I'd already freaked Ben out with boxing. He hadn't mentioned it, so I didn't either. I just kept my mouth shut all the way to the quarry, like a good girl.

The light from the flames of a big bonfire threw wild shadows against the rocks. Laughter drifted across the parking area.

Snow was falling again. Ben and Sam grinned at each other. "Party time!"

I pulled the hood of my jacket over my head.

"Hey, ladies. You just get here?" Megan handed us each a beer.

Alexis waved hers away. "I'll pass. I'm not feeling that great tonight."

Megan laughed. "Sam wearing you out?"

"Shut up, Megan," Alexis snapped.

"Must be her time of the month," Megan said to me in a mock whisper. "See you around, rag doll."

Alexis watched Megan saunter over to Ben and Sam. She put her arms around their waists.

"Could her shirt be cut any lower?" Alexis said.

"I know," I said. "Michael says she's a skank."

"Slut's more like it. But Michael's too nice a guy to say that."

Nice and *gay*. I'd been wanting to talk with Alexis about Michael. She'd known him practically as long as I had.

I took a sip of beer. "Speaking of Michael," I said.

But Alexis wasn't listening to me. She was calling to a group of kids I didn't know who'd just pulled up. "Catch up with you a little later, Mardie," she said, heading off in the other direction.

Sweat rolled down the small of my back. I shrugged out of my jacket and moved away from the noise, smoke, and heat.

Away from the fire, in the dark of the night, I could see just how hard it was snowing. I always liked snow, the clean quiet of it.

I remembered sledding at the top of Miners Hill with Michael when we were little. It seemed as big as Mount Everest then. I would sit in between Michael's legs, his arms around my waist. Dad would push us off and down we'd sail.

I drank another beer, wandered from group to group. Sam and Alexis talked with a pack of jocks and cheerleaders. Alexis laughed at something stupid one of the guys said. She glanced at me and said, "Can you *believe* that, Mardie?" Once again, I was on the outside.

I glanced down at my watch. Almost an hour since I'd seen Ben. Where was he? I caught Sam's eye. "You seen Ben?" I asked.

Someone passed Sam a joint. He took a deep hit and shook his head.

I wandered over to the edge of the water. It was cold

enough now that a thin skin of ice glinted in the shallow parts. This is where I'd met Ben on that hot summer day, not that long ago. Soon the water in the quarry would be frozen solid.

Raspy laughter floated from under a rocky outcropping. Megan. Probably with some guy.

Then I heard a low, familiar voice say, "God, that feels good."

I slipped over to get a better look. I almost puked.

Ben stood with his back against the rock wall. And there was Megan, magenta hair glowing in the firelight, Ben's hands moving under her shirt.

Rage flew over me. I grabbed a rock and hurled it at Ben. "You asshole!" I yelled. The rock hit him squarely on the forehead.

I don't know how far I ran down the long, dark road. How much farther was it to the bus stop? Another couple of miles? Three miles? Who cared? I just wanted to get as far away from Ben and Megan as I could.

I pulled my phone out of my pocket and called Michael's work number.

"I can't come get you this time, Mardie," he said.

"But, Michael," I sobbed. "I'm freezing!"

"I thought you and Ben were at a movie," he said.

"I'm not, okay? We were out at the quarry. I need you to come get me."

"Can't, Mardie. We're shorthanded tonight. I'm work-ing with the boss."

"Michael, please," I pleaded. "You were totally right about Ben."

Michael was quiet. "I'm sorry to hear that, little sis-ter," he said. "But I still can't bail you out."

My teeth shattered so hard I thought they'd break. Damn Michael. Damn Ben. Damn my stupid, stupid life. I stood in the falling snow and cried. There was nothing else to do. I called the house.

"Mardie?" Amy didn't even say hello. And how the hell did she know it was me?

"I need a ride home," I said.

"Why, what happened?"

"Ben and I had a fight. I need a ride home," I said.

"But if you went to the movies, you could easily catch the bus. So where are you?" Screwed again.

Amy turned up the heat in the car. Teddy and Max licked the side of my face. Finally Amy said, "The quarry?"

I nodded.

Amy sighed. "Mardie, honey, you are walking a path of self-destruction and I do *not* understand why."

I couldn't honestly say I did either. "Was Dad asleep?" I asked.

"Yep," Amy said. "That's why I brought the dogs, so they wouldn't bark when I left."

I relaxed. Maybe it wouldn't be so bad.

But then, "He'll have to know, though."

"Why?" I wailed. "I didn't hurt anybody!"

"You are hurting yourself, Mardie. You make your bed, you lie in it."

I sighed. There she went with that bed stuff again.

When we pulled up to the house, the lights were on in the front room. Dad was up.

"What's going on here?" he asked, looking from Amy to me. Amy tossed her keys on the hall table and shrugged out of her coat. She was in her pajamas. "Ask your daughter," she said.

"Mardie?" Dad said.

"It's no big deal, Dad. Ben and I got into a little fight. That's all. I needed a ride home."

"He wouldn't give you a ride home? In this weather?" Dad asked.

"They weren't at the movies, Dave," Amy said.

Dad's face turned red. The little vein in his temple jumped.

Here we go again.

"I'm grounded, needless to say," I said into the phone from underneath the covers. It was still snowing hard outside. The growl of snowblowers filled the morning air.

"I can't believe Ben did that to you, Mardie," Alexis said. "You really nailed him, though. He had blood all over his face. Everyone there was laughing at him."

Somehow, I took little comfort in that. My life as I knew it was over.

"And that slut, Megan," Alexis continued. "What kind of person is she anyway, to do something like that to a friend?"

"Not much of a friend, I guess," I said. "What did Sam say?"

Alexis sighed. "He was mad at Ben and chewed him out. But guys always stick with guys in the end."

There was a tap on my bedroom door. "Gotta go," I said.

Amy came in, followed by the dogs. Teddy jumped on the bed, nosing his way under the covers. "I want to talk with you about last night," she said, sitting on the desk chair.

She cleared her throat and said, "Mardie, did Ben hurt you last night?"

"What do you mean?"

"I mean," Amy said, "did he try to force you to do something you didn't want to do?"

"Oh, you mean like *sex*?"

"Yes, Mardie. Like sex."

I looked out the window. Dad was shoveling the front walk. "Did Dad tell you to ask me this?"

"No, he didn't. Quite frankly, your dad is so mad at you he doesn't trust himself to talk to you. This is *my* question."

"No, Ben didn't hurt me. Not physically anyway. He was too busy with someone else."

Amy shook her head. "What a jerk. I knew there was a reason I didn't like that guy."

"Don't worry, he got his. I nailed him really good with a rock."

Amy laughed. Then she said, "Mardie, I know it's tough being fifteen. So many things are changing and guys don't make it any easier. You can talk to me, you know."

I reached under the covers and scratched Teddy behind his ears.

Amy studied my face. "You used to talk to me all the time," she said. "I thought you'd never shut up. But now we never talk."

I shrugged.

"Well," she said getting up. "I'm worried about you, Mardie. And I'm here if you need me."

Part of me really wanted to talk to her about everything, just like I used to. But I didn't know how to put into words everything that was all tied up inside me. So I just picked at a spot on my comforter.

Amy put on her parent voice. "You need to get up and get dressed. There's a snow shovel on the deck with your name on it."

Later that night, Dad came into my room. His hands were in his pockets. He looked like he wanted to be anywhere but there. "Mardie," he said, "is there anything you want to talk about?"

"Like what, Dad?"

"I don't know. Like Ben. Like why guys are such jerks."

I picked up my pencil to give him a hint. "I'm doing calculus homework. I'm behind. Besides, Amy already had this little discussion with me, so you're off the hook."

Dad's face darkened. "You don't have to be so sarcastic, Mardie. We're worried about you."

"Well, stop worrying about me so much, Dad. You're driving me crazy. Besides, why would I talk to you about Ben?"

He shrugged. "Because I'm a guy?"

"God Dad, you're not a 'guy'! You're, like, my dad."

Okay, I was a little harsh. But the thought of talking with him about what happened with Ben and Megan was creepy.

I tried to pretend I was sick Monday morning. Dad didn't buy it. But it was true, really. The thought of the loser-looks in the hallways at school, the possibility of seeing Ben, actually made my stomach hurt.

I dreaded fourth-period English. Megan would be there. Megan and her magenta hair and big boobs. I hadn't seen Ben yet, but everyone was talking about the big knot on his head. "It looks like an Easter egg," Alexis said, laughing.

And sure enough, there Megan sat, slouched across from my desk. The classroom was unusually quiet. As I bent down to get my dictionary, Megan tried to pass me a note. "Fuck off," I said under my breath.

The bell for next class finally rang. I took a really long time putting my things into my backpack. Right after I stepped out into the hallway, though, I heard a familiar voice say, "Still friends?" I turned around. Megan smiled a slow, lazy smile. "Come on, girlfriend. Let's not let something silly like a boy ruin a beautiful friendship."

"Friends don't treat each other that way," I snapped.

Megan stepped closer and put a hand on my arm. "I warned you, didn't I? Guys like Ben aren't going to be satisfied with looks and a little hand-holding. You can't blame me."

All the rage and humiliation of the last few days exploded. I pushed Megan away, maybe a little too hard. "Hey!" Megan yelled. "What the hell!"

I grabbed the front of her shirt and slammed her against the locker. "You slut," I said. "You stay out of my face and out of my life or—"

A hand gripped my shoulder. "Let her go, Mardie. She's not worth getting suspended over."

Rick. He said again, "She's so not worth it, Mardie."

Tears stung my eyes. I unclenched my hand and stepped back.

"Bitch," Megan said, as she slid away.

I slumped against the wall. "Rick, I really—"

He picked up his books. "Let's go. We're going to be late to our next class."

Eight

I don't remember much about the next couple of weeks. When I try to think of that dark time, all I can remember is pain. Crashing pain like cinder blocks falling on me. I didn't sleep. The nights seemed like they'd never end. But then, I didn't want to get out of bed either. I just wanted my life to be over.

But it wasn't. Dad took me to school every morning, with a pat on the knee and a "Hang in there, bug."

I went to class. Avoided talking to anyone as much as possible. Not that people were exactly standing in line to talk to me. Now that I was no longer with Ben, I was once again an invisible nobody.

At lunch now, Alexis sat with her French Club or Journalism Club friends, leaving me to the Loser Zone. She invited me to sit with them a few times, but they all either looked right through me or had this snarky way of bringing Ben's name into the conversation. There are times when I truly think high school is a haven for cannibals.

Once or twice I ran into Shireen in the hall. She'd always smile wide, pop her gum, and say, "Where you been, Mardie? When you coming back to the gym?"

I couldn't imagine having the energy to go back there.

School would be out for most of the week for Thanksgiving. Usually I looked forward to that, being able to sleep late and spend the day just kicking around with Alexis. But she was going to Denver this year to visit her grandparents, so that was out.

And obviously, I wouldn't be seeing Ben. Wouldn't you think after everything that'd happened, he'd be the last person on earth I'd want to see, or even think about? But I did anyway.

The day before Thanksgiving was particularly boring. Everybody was either at work or out of town. Even the dogs were gone. They were at the groomers, getting their holiday baths. Nothing much on TV, except those stupid holiday shows and commercials.

I clicked off the TV and tossed the remote in Max's toy basket. A black, black mood descended like a thick fog. I wanted to go back to bed and just sleep until everything was . . . what? Different? But Amy would be home from work early, and if she caught me still in bed, she'd come up with some "character building" chores for me to do. I put on my coat, wound a thick scarf around my neck, and stepped out into the cold, thin sunlight. I caught the bus for the mall.

Looking back on it later, it seems like someone else's hand was doing it.

First that hand slipped a bottle of perfume into my pocket, then a tube of expensive lipstick. I wandered over to the electronics section of the store. Amazing how easy it was to slip those CDs into my pocket.

I pretended to be interested in the digital camera display, even went so far as to ask the salesperson which camera was best. But the cameras were kept behind the counter. Too bad. I pocketed a calculator instead.

The store lights were too bright, the buzz of voices made my head pound. But still, in there I felt more alive, more in control than I had in weeks.

My pockets were heavy. I walked over to the jewelry section. The more expensive things were in locked cases, but there were boxed sets of necklaces and matching earrings on table displays. Amy loved jewelry. I decided on a Celtic-looking silver necklace and earring set.

At the checkout, I paid for a pair of socks, the kind Dad likes. I took my bag. "Have a good one," I said, and headed for the doors. I grinned. Maybe I should join the Drama Club.

A voice stopped me dead in my tracks. "That's far enough, young lady." Heart sinking, I turned.

Two uniformed security guards stood there, frowning. Shoppers milled around them, looking at me curiously. A guard stepped forward, took my elbow. "Come with us, please."

The drive home from the department store was the longest in my life. Dad clenched and unclenched his jaw, regular as a metronome. Amy wrung the strap of her purse like a wet rag, probably wishing it was my neck. Neither of them said anything, but Dad's words still rung in my ears: "What is *wrong* with you, Mardie? Why are you doing this?"

When I tried to explain about how my hand wasn't my hand, and that it all seemed like someone else doing it, he went nuclear. "You are *just* like your mother! Never taking responsibility for *anything*! *Never* thinking about the consequences of your actions!"

The worst part, even worse than Dad's yelling, was Amy's silence. She just looked at me like I was the worst piece of shit she'd ever come across.

"Go to your room, Mardie. Amy and I need to talk."

"Can't I get a drink first, or is this going to be like prison, with only bread and water?"

Before Dad could react, Amy narrowed her eyes and spat back in the hardest voice I'd ever heard: "You are walking a thin line, young lady. Go to your room. Now!"

The wind pushed against the side of the house. Sleet tapped against my window. I held my mother's picture against my chest. She would have understood, wouldn't she? At least she wouldn't have looked at me like I was some kind of criminal. Maybe my mother would have . . .

Dad opened the bedroom door without knocking. "Amy and I need to talk to you, Mardie." I placed the picture on the bed.

Dad glanced at it, then turned away.

I followed him, like a condemned prisoner, to the living room.

"Mardie, can you explain to us why you stole those things?" Dad asked.

"I told you, I don't know," I said.

Amy sighed. "Mardie, it's not like you don't have control over your actions."

"I said I don't *know*! I was bored, I went to the mall. I thought I'd look for Christmas presents."

"And instead, you stole them," Amy said flatly.

"I just took a few stupid things, okay? It's not like I robbed a bank."

"How's it that much different, Mardie?" Dad said. "You were arrested. You now have a record. You have an appointment before a judge in a week." His voice rising, he continued, "It's been one thing after another! First that party and the police. Then telling us you were going to the movies but instead you go out to the quarry, doing who-knows-what. And now, shoplifting. What the hell is going on with you, Mardie?"

"Like you really care, Dad! Like you really want to know what I feel!"

"We do, Mardie," Amy said.

"No you don't," I said. "All *you* care about are your precious dogs and Michael. And all Dad cares about is keeping things status quo. Let's not rock the boat. Let's never look back. And for god's sake don't talk about their mother. Unless, of course, it's to tell Mardie what a fuckup she is, because she's just like her."

Dad looked like I'd slapped him right in the face. He looked away.

Amy said, "We care very much about you, Mardie. We're angry with you, yes, but more than that, we're worried about you. You are so angry, and we don't understand why."

"What a surprise," I said.

"Yes, it *is* a surprise. What is it you want? Why do you think you have it so terrible? For the life of me, I cannot figure out—"

The front door opened. "Hey! Look at you all! What a great family!" Michael stood in the living room grinning, snow in his hair, arms encircling a phantom, perfect family.

Michael looked from face to face. His arms lowered to his side. "Okay, so maybe not the happiest family right at the moment," he said, as he edged toward the stairs.

There was Michael, always the perfect son. Look how wonderful Michael's grades are! Look at Michael, captain of the lacrosse team! Look at Michael—just like Dad.

"You think Michael's so perfect. You think Michael is the golden boy, this perfect son," I said.

Michael stopped, one foot on the third stair. He shot me a warning look.

"Now listen," Dad said. "This is not about Michael. Don't try and blame—"

"Blame, Dad?" I said. "You accuse me of sneaking around, of lying. Maybe you should ask Michael about *his* secrets!"

Dad looked at Michael, eyebrows raised.

I narrowed my eyes and sneered. I *hated* myself, absolutely hated myself as I said it: "Go ahead, Michael, tell them. Tell them you're gay."

NINE

I lay in bed early the next morning listening for the usual sound of happy chaos: Dad singing as he made pancakes, the clatter of pots and pans as Amy looked for the giant roasting pan they used only once a year. The Macy's Thanksgiving Day Parade blaring from the TV set, Michael singing an aria to the turkey. There was something I loved about the craziness in the kitchen.

But not this Thanksgiving. It was eerily, sadly quiet. All because of me.

Footsteps padded down the stairs. Pots and pans clattered. The sliding glass door opened. Teddy barked at the scrub jays in the backyard. Amy was up.

I pulled on sweatpants and an old sweatshirt. I glanced in the mirror. I looked like hell. I grabbed my hair and tied it back in a severe braid.

Amy didn't look much better. Dark circles shadowed her eyes, her red hair pushed back haphazardly. She barely glanced up when I came in the kitchen.

I took the copper kettle off the stove and filled it with water. "You going to want some tea?" I asked.

Amy looked over her shoulder. "Sure," she said.

"I'll put enough in for Michael, too," I said. Amy raised one eyebrow and went on searching through the cabinets.

I cleared my throat. "I think I saw the roasting pan in that bottom cabinet in the pantry," I offered. "Do you want me to look?"

Amy eyed me for a long second. "That would be helpful," she said.

The kettle whistled. I reached two cups down from the cupboard and turned off the burner. I pawed through the big wicker basket where Amy and Michael kept their tea. Darjeeling, Ceylon, Earl Grey, Asaam, Lapsang Souchong, Jasmine . . . who knew what to drink?

Amy reached around and plucked a packet of Lapsang Souchong from the basket. I followed her lead. We poured the steaming water into the cups, over the bags. A sharp, smoky smell filled the kitchen.

I sipped my tea and coughed. "Tastes like a campfire," I said.

Amy pushed the honey over. "Since when did you become a tea drinker? I thought you were a coffee gal."

"Just thought I'd try something different." I stirred a huge spoonful of honey into my tea.

"Seems you're doing a lot of that lately," Amy said.

The day didn't get any easier. Everyone was busy avoiding each other's eyes, being polite.

Michael spent an inordinate amount of time shoveling the six inches of wet snow that had fallen overnight. Dad helped the old couple two houses down shovel their drive and walkway. Then he shoveled everyone else's sidewalk.

Dad cooked and cooked, Amy cleaned and cleaned. She grabbed the leashes off the hook by the front door. "I'm going to get these guys out for a walk," she said.

"I can take them," I said from the couch.

Amy looked doubtful. "I don't know what your dad and I have decided yet about letting you out."

"Well, I can't go inside anywhere with the dogs," I said.

Amy fidgeted with the leashes. "I guess they could be your chaperones," she said. "But take a watch with you and be back in an hour. The turkey will be ready at four. One of your dad's students is coming at three-thirty."

Most every year, at least one of Dad's students came to our house for Thanksgiving dinner. These were students who lived too far away to go home for the short Thanksgiving break and had nowhere else to go. Sometimes they were from back East somewhere, but more often they were from other countries. Why someone from Spain or Iran would want to go to school at little Western Colorado University is beyond me. They probably couldn't get into good universities in their own country. Still, it was kind of interesting sometimes.

The golden brown turkey squatted on the silver platter in the center of the dining room table. When we were little, Amy let us make these colorful, tasseled paper sleeves to outfit the ends of the drumsticks. But we hadn't done that for a long time.

Dad cleared his throat. "You all know we have a lot to be thankful for as a family." Dad made this speech every year. Part of the Thanksgiving tradition. Then everyone, even the homeless student, went around the table and said one thing they were thankful for.

One year Michael said he was thankful he didn't live in a concentration camp. That was when he was ten and obsessed with the Nazis.

Rumor had it that when I was six, I said I was thankful I wasn't God. I still don't know why everyone thinks that's such a hilarious story.

This year, Dad forgot this part of the tradition.

The student's name was Dylan. Dylan McTavish. And he was the palest person I'd ever seen. He was from some little town on the northern coast of Scotland. His hair was black and looked like he'd cut it himself with fingernail scissors. He had a tiny silver cross in his left earlobe.

I could barely understand a word he said. I gathered from Michael's end of the conversation that they were talking politics and sports. Dylan moved saltshakers and candleholders around, trying to explain cricket to us.

In the lull between turkey and Amy's famous sweet potato pie, Dylan said, "And what do you do, Mardie?" *Do?*

"Get arrested and embarrass my family."

Dylan laughed. Dad glared. Amy said, with a little too much enthusiasm, "Mardie's in tenth grade."

"And how is that for you, Mardie?" Dylan asked.

"It sucks," I said. He nodded.

"Big-time," I clarified.

Dad cleared his throat. "Mardie's just having a little trouble finding her way." He was right. I was like a tourist without a map to my own life.

Then out of the blue, Michael said, "Actually, she's an athlete." We all looked at Michael like he'd said, "Actually, she's the Virgin Mary."

"Really? And what sport would you be playing?" Dylan asked.

Amy, Dad, and I looked at Michael.

"She boxes."

Dylan sat up a little straighter. He studied me like I might actually be interesting.

"She's pretty good, too," Michael said, like he had watched me spar a million times.

"Cool," Dylan said.

Dad sighed. I grinned.

Later that night, after Michael took Dylan back to the dorms, I managed to get him alone in the kitchen.

"Thanks, Michael."

"For what?"

"You know, for telling Dylan about the boxing."

Michael shrugged and turned his back to me.

"Why did you say I was good?"

"You've always been good at sports."

"Yeah, but you've never even seen me in the ring. But maybe sometime—"

Michael turned around. His eyes hit me hard. "Just because I steered the conversation away from your screwups doesn't mean I'm not mad at you."

I felt like he'd sucker punched me in the stomach. "Oh, come on, Michael."

He brushed past me. "End of conversation, Mardie."

Saturday night, late, Michael came in from work, his soft voice greeting the dogs. The refrigerator door opened, then closed. I took a deep breath. It was time.

"So are you ever going to speak to me again?" I asked, leaning one hip on the counter.

"That's still up for debate," Michael said. He tossed each of the dogs a piece of cold turkey. Teddy caught his in midair with a snap. Max was hopeless.

"Well, maybe you could write me a note when you want to tell me something," I said. "Like that time when we were little and pretended we were mutes." I thought the memory would make Michael smile. And then, once he smiled, the ice would be broken and I could tell him how sorry I was for my big, fat mouth.

But he didn't.

"If I wrote you a note, I'd tell you to stay the hell out of my business," he snapped. "That part of my life is nobody's business but mine."

"If you're so ashamed of it, Michael, then why not be normal?"

He glared at me. "I'm not ashamed! And I *am* normal."

Okay, he wasn't making apologizing easy. "If you're so proud of it, then why keep it such a big secret?"

Michael shook his head. "God, Mardie, you sound like those idiots you've been hanging out with. I'm gay. So what? Why should I tell everyone?"

"Then why are you so pissed I broke your little secret to Dad and Amy?"

Michael sighed. "You've given them plenty of other things to worry about lately. I didn't want to add to it."

I turned to leave. It was no use. Why should I apologize? No matter what I did, Michael managed to come out of it the shining example.

Then I stopped. "I don't believe you, Michael. You've been avoiding Dad and Amy like the plague, ever since I outed you. You're just like the rest of us. You have no friggin' idea who you are."

TEN

Here's number one on the top-ten reasons I hate living in a small town: everyone knows your business. The way everyone avoided me at school on Monday, you'd think I'd been caught robbing a bank or selling drugs to kindergartners, rather than lifting a few stupid things from a department store.

Even Alexis went off the radar. Amazing how she was never home or was in the shower whenever I called. Somehow, I didn't believe her. When I saw her at school, she was hanging all over Sam, who was usually with Ben. Not a good equation. My life totally sucked on a whole new level.

And just like when I was a kid, I had to go to the public library after school where Amy works. When Dad dropped me off at school that morning, he said, "We can't trust you, Mardie, so you'll need to go straight to the library after school and wait for Amy until she gets off. Then we need to head over to the courthouse to meet with the judge."

I found a table over by the big bay windows. Two frigging hours until Amy was off from work. Crap. I took my copy of *To Kill a Mockingbird* out of my backpack and flipped to Chapter Twelve. I sighed. Seemed like Scout and I were always getting in trouble.

I sat in the leather chair across from Judge Martinez's huge desk, feeling really small. Dad's leg jiggled up and down like it always does when he's nervous. I wasn't expecting a female judge, much less a young one. Maybe she'd be cool and not come down too hard.

Judge Martinez sighed, closing the file. She looked at me way too long. I squirmed in my chair. Then she said, "What's going on with you, Mardie?"

I looked to Dad and Amy.

Amy started to say something, but the judge cut her off. "I'm asking Mardie."

I shrugged. "I don't know."

Judge Martinez reopened the file. She glanced down at the report, then said in a clipped voice, "You have no *idea* why you stole ninety-three dollars' worth of merchandise from Brannigan's?" She flipped back a couple of pages. "And you have no *idea* why you were taken to the police station in September for drunken and disorderly conduct?" she asked.

The judge asked my parents, "How are her grades?"

"Her grades stink," Dad said. "Mardie's always been a decent student. This year she's not trying. At all."

"We've caught her sneaking out of the house. She's

lied to us on several occasions. At least that we know about," Amy added, like I wasn't even there.

The judge tapped her scarlet fingernail on the desk. She leaned toward me. "Mardie, I see far too many girls your age come through this court. Like you, they're smart, have advantages some kids can only dream about. And like you, they have no idea what they are so pissed off about and what it is they want."

My eyes burned, but I'd be damned if I'd cry.

The judge leaned back, scribbling something in the file. "You'll be on one year's probation. If you so much as steal a pack of mints or annoy the neighbors playing your music too loud, I'll put you in juvie so fast it will make your head spin. You will also repay Brannigan's for the merchandise you stole. And you can never set foot in that department store again."

I looked down at my hands. I couldn't imagine going back there anyway. Everyone would be watching me.

Judge Martinez continued, "Furthermore, I'm ordering you to do one hundred hours of community service. You will also pay the courts a fine in the sum of two hundred dollars."

Silence.

"Is that all, Your Honor?" Dad asked.

The judge nodded. "I'll expect to see you again in three months. By that point, Mardie, you should be well into your community service."

I just nodded.

Standing, she said to Amy and Dad, "If she sneaks out of the house, report it to the police. She'll be a runaway."

The next day after school, I sat at the same table in the library.

I looked at the list of places I could do community service: the Humane Society, Catholic Mission Services, Community Recycling, the Ronald McDonald House, the New Horizons Center, South Eden Public Library, and several more equally depressing choices.

"Hey, Mardie," a familiar voice said. It was Rick. He wheeled a book cart over.

"Oh hey," I said. "What are you doing here?"

"I work here a couple days a week, shelving books and stuff."

How incredibly normal.

"What's that you got there?" he asked.

"Seems I have to do a hundred hours of community service as part of my punishment for my life of crime. This is a list of places I can do it." I slid the paper across the table.

"Oh hey, the New Horizons Center. That would be a good place." He sat down.

"You're kidding, right?" I said. "I don't want to spend a hundred hours changing diapers on drooling freaks."

Rick flushed. The muscle in his jaw tightened.

"I volunteer there a couple times a week. And trust me, I'm not 'changing diapers on drooling freaks.'"

Great. "And why on earth would you be there voluntarily?"

"Because," Rick said, "my sister goes there every day."

"She works there?" I asked.

"No," Rick said. "She's one of those 'diaper-wearing drooling freaks.' "

"Oh crap, Rick. I'm sorry! What an idiot."

"It's okay," Rick said.

We were both quiet for a few awkward seconds. Then I asked, "So why do you go there, and what do you do?"

Rick shrugged, looking down at his hands. "Well, my sister, Lizzie, has Down syndrome. And, I don't know, I like being there with her. And with the other people, too. It's hard to explain. You'd have to come see for yourself. Why don't you come by on Saturday? I can show you around."

"I don't know," I said.

Rick's face flushed. He stood up and started to wheel his book cart away.

"On the other hand," I said, "it's one way to get out of the prison my family calls home."

Rick grinned. "Great. We're usually there from nine to four."

Ever since my fall from grace, dinner at home had become very quiet. Conversation used to bounce around the table, going from lacrosse, to tenth-century Asian history, to the funny thing a three-year-old had said to Amy, and then back again. Getting a word in edgewise usually was totally impossible.

But tonight, when I cleared my throat at the table, it was as loud as a gunshot.

Everyone looked at me like I'd stood up and started singing the "Star Spangled Banner" in the middle of a prayer service.

"So I think I'm going to do my community service at the New Horizons Center."

Dad's eyebrows about shot off the top of his head. Michael squinted at me like a bug. "You? You're kidding."

Amy took a deep breath. "It may not be the easiest place, Mardie."

Duh.

"Could you take me there on Saturday to check it out?" I asked.

"I'm working Saturday," Amy said.

"Dad?"

"Sure," Dad said. "Saturday it is."

And that was all anybody said.

The head person for that day at New Horizons shuffled through my court papers, and then he pulled out a bright yellow file labeled COMMUNITY SERVICE. It might as well have been labeled TOTAL LOSERS. They'd probably have me scrubbing toilets with a toothbrush and leave the fun jobs to the noncriminal volunteers.

Mr. Head Person leaned back in his chair and studied me. "One hundred hours, huh?"

Dad's face turned red.

I wanted the floor to open up and swallow me whole. It didn't, so I just nodded. "Yes, sir."

He tapped his pen on the file folder, probably trying to decide what was the worst he could do to me. Then he said, "I have a daughter about your age." *Tap, tap, tap.*

Then he said, "You have any experience with horses?"

Horses? Did he say *horses?* "Excuse me?" I asked.

"We have a very active riding program here, with ten horses and students with all kinds of abilities. Pete Ruskin is the head instructor. Great guy, but he can always use some help." *Tap, tap, tap.* "You interested?"

I couldn't believe my ears. *Horses!* "Yes, sir," I said. "I used to ride all the time."

"Well then, we're all set. I'll walk you over to the stables and get you going with Pete. He may have you muck out stalls and clean the tack. I don't know that you'll do any actual riding. At least not for a while."

Great.

Dad glanced at me. "She'll do anything you need her to do. Without complaint. Right, Mardie?"

I guess when you're a convicted felon, you can't exactly complain about shoveling shit.

"Sure," I said.

Head Guy gave us a tour around the place. It was actually pretty impressive.

There was an indoor climbing wall, ski outings, time on the computers, crafts, music. In the summer, they had a whole different program. As we passed the computer lab on the way to the indoor stables, I saw Rick working with a guy in a wheelchair and waved hello.

When we entered the stables, the smell of horse and poop and leather and straw brought back a whole boatload of memories.

Call me crazy, but I love the smell. Which was a good thing because those first three Saturdays, that's what I mostly did: shovel horse poop and pitch straw. The only good thing about it was by the end of the day, I was too tired to wonder what Alexis and Sam and Ben and everyone else in the real world had done that Saturday.

By the fourth Saturday, though, Pete said, "How would you like a break from mucking today?"

A pathetic thrill ran through me. "Sure," I said.

"Great," Pete said. "I could use help with students."

I nodded.

"Our first one this morning is a little girl named Hannah. Severe case of cerebral palsy. I have to lift her into the saddle, and my back's acting up." He looked me over. "You're tall and look fairly strong."

Nothing like slinging around shovels full of shit to buff out. "I can hold my own," I said.

Waving at a man pushing a wheelchair toward us, he said, "Good. Here she comes."

The small girl in the chair flopped to one side like a rag doll, but her face was split with the biggest smile I'd ever seen.

Pete and I carefully positioned Hannah in the saddle atop Feather, the little gray gelding. The horse stood patiently as we adjusted stirrups and positioned the reins in Hannah's hand. Her head lolled loosely on her neck, and she had control of only one hand. She drooled, and it was kind of hard to understand what she said.

I took a deep breath. What had I gotten myself into?

"Okay, Hannah, Feather's chomping at the bit and so are you. You ready to ride?" Pete asked.

She nodded.

"Then let's head 'em up and move 'em out!"

I walked beside Feather's head, leading him by a rope. Pete walked beside Hannah, keeping her steady in the saddle. Pete told me the trick was to give Hannah just enough support so she wouldn't slide out of the saddle, but also to force her to use her own muscles to stay upright as much as possible.

"When Hannah first started riding lessons, she couldn't stay on for more than a couple minutes before her muscles gave out. Now she can ride a full fifteen minutes before her muscles start to quiver." Pride lit Pete's face.

By the end of fifteen minutes, Hannah was done. I helped Pete lift her off the horse and into her father's arms. Her shirt and hair were wet and she smelled like pee. I hated how squeamish I felt.

Another one of my jobs that day was helping with lunch. Most of the people could feed themselves, but a few couldn't.

"How'd Hannah do in the ring today?" Rick asked, sitting down beside me. He carefully wiped the corner of Kaitlin's mouth. She grinned hugely.

"Um, awesome," I replied, spooning applesauce into Roger's mouth. Would I ever get used to this?

"She rode fifteen minutes today. She wanted to stay on longer, but Pete said she'd wear Feather out." I spooned more applesauce into Roger's open mouth. Half of it spilled out. A grown man with applesauce running down the side of his face was not a pretty sight. But nobody else seemed to care.

After lunch came the indoor climbing wall. This was Rick's specialty, and Lizzie's—his sister's—all-time favorite thing to do.

The first time I met Lizzie, I felt weird around her. It was like she had a grown woman's body, but inside she was more like a four-year-old. It had been Lizzie's room, filled with stuffed animals and dolls, I'd seen that night at Rick's party.

Now, after four visits to New Horizons, I didn't stiffen when Lizzie and some of the other students hugged me. They were just who they were, without any apologies. And that was okay with me.

ELEVEN

Monday night. Dad and I cleared the table and loaded the dishes in the dishwasher while Amy talked with her sister in Georgia. She'd been on the phone for a long time. When she came out of the study, she said, "Listen up, little family of mine, we're doing something different this year for Christmas."

"Like what?" Dad asked.

"We're going to Georgia," Amy announced, grinning.

"I don't know, honey," Dad said. "That's a long trip and it'll be expensive for all of us to fly."

Amy crossed her arms over her chest, sticking her chin out. "Dave, when was the last time we spent a holiday with my kin in my hometown?"

"Well—," Dad said, rubbing the back of his neck.

Amy cut him off. "Never, Dave. That's the last time. We're not poor, for god's sake, and we could all use a change of scenery this year."

I turned back to the dishwasher. Dad didn't stand a chance. Amy had made up her mind. And when Amy makes up her mind, that's pretty much it.

Michael came in the front door, sweaty from lacrosse practice.

"Hey, Michael," I said. "We're going to Georgia for Christmas."

Michael still wasn't talking to me much, so he asked Dad, "Why Georgia?"

"Why *not* Georgia?" Amy asked.

Michael rooted around in the fridge for leftovers. "How long would we be gone?"

"I don't know," Dad said. "Christmas is on Thursday this year, so I would imagine at least four or five days. Why?"

Michael frowned. "Because I don't think I can get that much time off work. I'll just stay here and look after Max and Teddy. Dylan will be around, too. He'll need somebody to hang out with."

Dylan? The Scottish guy? Was he gay, too?

I was shocked when Amy said, "No, sir, you will not. You're coming with us." I'd never heard Amy use that tone of voice with Michael. Only with me.

"But Mom—"

"No buts," Amy said. "You have rarely ever missed a day at the radio station. Certainly not on holidays." Then a bit more gently she said, "We need to do something different together as a family, Michael. You'll be off to college next year, and everything will change."

As for me, I could use some change. My afternoon ritual was boring and always the same: come home from school, eat a yogurt, change clothes, leash up the dogs and walk them until suppertime. Pretty pathetic, I know, but what else did I have to do?

At first, Amy invited me along to the gym when she went. "I thought you enjoyed boxing," she'd say. But I just couldn't bring myself to go back there, not with this huge L on my forehead.

And even though I felt like Alexis had totally blown me off, I still missed her. I've never been one of those girls with a jillion friends. I've always gone more for quality over quantity. Still, I missed her crazy laugh and her even crazier ideas. I missed how much we knew about each other. Or at least we used to. Now, these four-footed, furry goofballs were my only friends.

So I leashed the dogs and walked all the way up to Main Street. Everything was decked out for the holidays. Strings of colored lights zigzagged above the street, creating a dizzying web of color. People dashed in and out of shops, laughing or looking totally stressed out, their cheeks red from the cold December wind.

Smitty's had a HELP WANTED sign in the window. Alexis and I used to save up our allowance, then come to Smitty's for burgers, fries, and as many games of pool as we had quarters for. When was the last time we'd done that?

I heard someone call my name. Shireen ran across the street.

"Hey, you! Where've you been? We miss you at the gym!"

"Right," I said.

"For true, *chica*. Kitty keeps looking at the door and saying, 'Where's Miss Mardie?' And Destiny and I don't have anybody good to spar with."

I bent down and pretended to untangle the leashes. "I've been busy with stuff. You know how it is."

"Yeah, especially this time of year. But still, we need you to come back. You're good, Mardie. Besides, you're the only normal one among us."

I laughed. "*Me?* The normal one?"

Shireen ticked off the abbreviated stories on her fingers: "Suze's mom is in and out of some kind of rehab every other week; Trish's uncle raped her sister. Oh, and Chris got pregnant. I don't even have a life because I have to take care of my little brother and sister all the time, and then, of course, there's Destiny."

I did miss how good I felt at the gym, how no one there cared about what a fuckup I was everywhere else. I even missed crunches and pushups.

Shireen brushed a lock of hair from my face, a surprisingly gentle gesture. "Come on, *chica*. We need you. You balance us out."

I looked away. "I don't feel very 'balanced' lately."

"Look, Mardie, if you're worried about the shoplifting stuff, who cares? You think any one of us down there is going to win South Eden's Good Citizen Award? We got no apologies and neither do you."

She continued, talking ninety miles an hour. "And the Rocky Mountain Women's Golden Gloves is coming up in June. Kitty thinks you and I have the best chance to be real contenders for the junior's title. But we got to start training hard, girlfriend, if we're gonna give it our best shot. We got to help each other out." Shireen popped her gum. "What do you say, *chica*?"

"I don't know," I said. "Let me consult with my learned advisors here. Teddy, Max, what do you think? Should I go hang at the gym with a bunch of other misfits?" Max barked and Teddy waved his tail. "My committee says 'yes.' "

Shireen laughed.

That night as Amy headed upstairs to bed, I called up after her, "Hey, Amy? Any chance I can catch a ride with you to the gym tomorrow night?"

She smiled. "Absolutely."

I couldn't believe how crazy busy my life became after that. Two hours of training every Tuesday and Thursday night, and most every Friday night, too. Saturdays I was at New Horizons all day, and Sundays I was trying to get caught up on my schoolwork.

Dad let me start boxing again on the condition that I brought my grades up and kept them there. Nothing lower than a C. I had a pretty serious hole to dig myself out of by the Christmas break.

At the gym Thursday night, I said, "Hey, Kitty, when do I get to start actually fighting?"

"There's plenty of time for that. You still got a ways to go."

"But you said the other night that I'm doing a lot better."

" 'A lot better' and 'ready for a fight' are two entirely different things, my friend. As I've told you before, there's a big difference between sparring and actually boxing. Right now, you wouldn't last three minutes in the ring with my grandmother."

That stung. "That's not true," I said. "You said I'm the strongest girl my age at the gym, but you let Shireen and Suze fight."

Kitty finished wrapping my hands and stood. "And they been coming here a lot longer than you. Be patient."

I stepped to the heavy bag and pictured Ben. I peppered the bag with a fast combination of jabs. I glanced at Kitty.

She smiled. "Impressive. But part of being a good boxer is patience, not just being able to beat the crap out of somebody. Which you obviously want to do in the worst way."

Before I could reply, Destiny appeared at Kitty's elbow. "I'll go in with her," she said.

Kitty raised her eyebrows. "What do you think, Mardie? You want to go in the ring with Destiny?"

I hesitated. Then I shrugged. "Why not?"

"Promise me you won't hurt Mardie," Kitty said to Destiny.

Helmets on and mouthpieces in. Kitty tied the laces of Destiny's gloves, then mine.

Destiny slipped between the ropes into the ring.

I followed, tripping on the lower rope. *Shit.*

Destiny looked even more intimidating with her helmet and gloves on. My mouth went dry. Suddenly, this didn't seem like such a great idea.

"Now remember, Mardie. Keep your hands up, chin tucked, and your weight balanced. The best offense is a good defense when you're up against someone bigger and more experienced. And keep moving! Destiny, go easy on her. Stay away from her head and face."

Destiny and I stood facing each other in the ring. Even though I'm way taller than she is, I felt like a little kid. All I could see of Destiny's face were her eyes—dark and hard like a shark's—and her mouth.

I gulped and tried to smile around my mouthpiece.

"Mix it up, ladies," Kitty called from the side of the ring.

Destiny bounced around me on her toes, light as a butterfly. I shuffled this way and that like my feet were encased in concrete.

Destiny threw a light jab at my shoulder. I threw up my gloves in front of my face.

"Don't just stand there, Mardie," Kitty called. "Fight!"

I swung at Destiny's right shoulder. She danced away, then popped me on the side of my helmet.

That pissed me off.

I shook off the punch and stormed in after her. I stuck her with a jab to her stomach, then followed with a left uppercut. That one actually landed.

But I didn't have too long to enjoy the look of surprise on her face because she caught me with my hands down and nailed me. I staggered to my knees.

Kitty rang the bell. She slipped between the ropes and pulled me to my feet. "You had enough?"

I nodded. I looked at the clock. I'd barely lasted two minutes with Destiny. And I was wasted. Totally trashed.

Kitty took my mouthpiece out. "So what do you think?" she asked as she untied my gloves.

I rubbed a sore place on my shoulder. "Seemed like everything I've learned just flew right out of my head," I said. "I forgot my combinations and my footwork."

"And you forgot to keep your hands up," Kitty said.

I shook my hair loose. "I think I even forgot to breathe."

"You landed a couple decent shots, though," Kitty said.

"I forgot she's a leftie," Destiny said from the bench.

"Well, the good thing is you don't seem glove shy. Even after Destiny popped you in the chin, you didn't back off."

I shook my head. "I was awful. I forgot everything you've taught me."

Kitty laughed as she unlaced my gloves. "Destiny would make any white girl forget her mama's name."

Later, after we finished crunches, I was in the locker room changing into warmer clothes when I heard, "You need to run."

I jumped. Jesus Christ. Why did Destiny have to sneak up on people like that?

I took a deep breath to calm my hammering heart. "I need to *what*?"

"Run. You need to run," Destiny said.

"I hate running," I said. "It's boring."

"Up to you," Destiny said. "But if you want to do anything in the ring, you run. Every day. Hard."

"So you run every day?" I asked.

Destiny pulled torn sweats over her shorts and zipped up her thin coat. "Yep, every day. Rain or shine. Sleet or snow."

I laughed, "Just like the U.S. post office, huh?"

Destiny smiled. "Just like the friggin' post office."

On the ride home, I closed my eyes. I could feel every spot where Destiny had landed a blow. Shoulders, chest, forearms, stomach. I'd be black and blue tomorrow. But remembering the feeling of throwing one or two perfect punches, seeing Destiny's eyes widen, it was worth it.

I was pretty much caught up in all my classes now. Maybe my grades wouldn't suck too bad after all.

As I hurried to my bus, I saw Alexis and Sam walking toward me, arms around each other.

"Uh-oh, there's Mardie," Sam said. "Hide your wallet!"

My face burned. "Very funny," I said, looking at Alexis. She just looked away. I couldn't believe it. How many times had I stood up for her when the other kids teased her?

"Hey, Al. You want to go to Smitty's?" I asked without looking at Sam.

She glanced at me and then at Sam. "Um, I don't—"

Sam tightened his grip on her. "She's busy. With me."

What was the matter with Alexis? "Can't she speak for herself?" I said.

"Maybe she doesn't want to speak to you," Sam said.

I looked at Sam, then at Alexis. "Is that true?"

Alexis shrugged. A shrug that summed up everything between us the last two months.

"That's just great, Alexis. Way to be." I pushed past them, bumping Alexis's shoulder. Hard. If Sam hadn't had his arm around her, she would have fallen.

Dusk. I leashed up the dogs for their afternoon walk. I was still angry, and sad, and depressed as hell about that shrug from Alexis. I needed to get out and do something.

The days were so short this time of year. It was pitch-dark by the time we headed for home. I decided to shortcut it across Silver Queen Park. I unleashed Teddy and Max for a few last minutes of freedom.

Two tall figures stood in the gazebo, passing something back and forth. Curious, I stepped a little closer, being careful to stay in the shadows. Then I heard a nauseatingly familiar voice say, "Yeah man, she'll do anything I ask. It's like having a pet dog." My heart raced. Ben. Ben and Eric Lindstrom. Eric said something I couldn't quite catch. But it was clear what he'd asked when Ben said, "Sure bro, I'll ask her. Like I said, she'll do anything. And it *is* the season of giving."

They made me sick. I backed quietly away. No way did I want them to see me.

Then Eric's voice stopped me dead in my tracks. "What have we here? It's a little foo-foo doggy."

It was Teddy still looking fine in his post-grooming ribbons. Teddy who wouldn't hurt a fly. Teddy who even considered the meter reader guy his friend. There he stood in the gazebo, waving his feathery tail, sure that Ben and Eric had a pocketful of treats.

I held my breath. Maybe they'd ignore him and Teddy would go away. I thought about calling him to me, but I was afraid of those two. I was caught between staying and running away.

Eric knelt down, saying in a sickeningly sweet voice, "Come here you little faggot dog. Come to Daddy. Let me show you what I have for dogs like you."

I stepped out of the shadows. "Touch him and I'll kill you," I said.

Ben spun around.

Eric rocked back on his heels, clutching Teddy by his collar. His pale hair glowed like silver, his blue eyes glittering hard as ice. "Well, look who's here. I should have known this queer-dog belonged to you. Or your brother."

Stepping closer, my heart racing, I said, "I mean it, Eric. Let him go." Eric threw back his head and laughed, braying like a donkey.

Teddy squirmed free of Eric's hands.

Ben reached down, grabbing him. Teddy yelped.

"Hey!" I yelled, stepping forward.

"I'm just trying to—" Ben's excuse was cut short.

Max came roaring out of the shadows. He hit Ben full force and knocked him backward. "Get him off me!" Ben screamed.

Eric whirled and started kicking Max.

Everything became crystal clear for me. All I'd learned sparring and hitting the mitts with Kitty clicked. When Eric swung his leg back to kick Max again, I caught him off balance. I grabbed his coat sleeve, spinning him around. He got the receiving end of my famous combination. I threw a wicked left hook that caught him under his chin, then a straight right to the nose. There was a boney pop. Blood squirted from his nose like a fountain. He doubled over. "My nose! The bitch broke my nose!"

I heard Kitty's voice in my ear, "Stick and run, Mardie. Stick and run!" I grabbed Teddy and yelled for Max. For the first time in his life, he actually obeyed. I ran as fast as I could, all the way home.

I flung myself in the front door and collapsed on the floor. My lungs felt like they were going to explode. Destiny was right: I needed to run. And my left hand hurt like hell.

Michael looked up from his place on the sofa. His eyes grew huge. He dropped the remote he had pointed at the TV screen.

He rushed over to us. "Christ, Mardie, what the hell's going on? Are you okay?"

I looked up at him, cradling my left hand. Eric's blood spattered the sleeve of my coat. "I think I just broke Eric Lindstrom's nose."

We sat on the kitchen floor. I held a bag of frozen peas

against my throbbing hand. Michael gently but carefully checked both dogs over for injuries. Maxie's side seemed tender, but Michael didn't think any bones were broken. Teddy was mostly shaken up.

Michael leaned back against the refrigerator and shook his head. "So. You really think you broke his nose?"

"Judging by the sound it made and all the blood, I'd say that's a yes."

Michael laughed for the first time in a long time. "You never cease to amaze me, little sister." Then he shook his head. "But that was a stupid thing to do. Eric's not only an asshole, he's a mean asshole. He's famous for holding grudges. He won't let this go, Mardie."

"You would have done the same thing, Michael. He hurt Teddy."

He handed me another bag of frozen veggies. "I don't know. Eric scares me. He'd love an excuse to beat the hell out of a queer." I'd never heard Michael talk like that before.

The garage door opened. Dad and Amy were home. As Michael helped me up off the floor, he said, "Just watch your back, Mardie. Eric's going to have it in for you big-time now."

News travels fast in a small town, especially in a high school. Everyone was talking about Eric's broken nose the next day. Kids in the halls at school, most of whom I didn't even know, either gave me a thumbs-up or went way around me, eyeing me like I was a crazy person.

At lunch, the noise in the cafeteria lowered to a dull roar when I walked in. The Cheerleader Table tittered. The

Jock Table grumbled. And there was a smattering of shy applause from the Geek, Vegan, and Suffering Artists tables.

Shireen rushed over from one of several Latino tables. "*Chica!* You are awesome!" she said, giving me a high five. She led me over to her group. "You are totally my hero, girlfriend!" she said. I nodded at the other kids sitting there. The girls smiled and introduced themselves. Even the guys nodded with a polite, grudging respect. It felt good. I finally had a place at the table.

It was a different story at training that night. Kitty's eyes followed me as I walked over to the heavy bag. She was not smiling.

"Mardie, I need to talk to you," she said.

"What's up?" I asked as I started wrapping my hand.

She grabbed my left hand and pointed to the bruises. "This," she said.

I pulled my hand away from her. "I didn't have any choice, Kitty. He started it."

She shook her head. "You sound like a little kid. 'He started it.' Except you're not a little kid, Mardie. I heard you broke his nose."

"Yeah, I did," I said.

Kitty sighed. "You know the rules, Mardie. Anyone fights outside of this ring is suspended from training. Indefinitely."

"Oh come *on*, Kitty," I said. "I told you it wasn't—"

"Your fault. I know. Listen, Mardie, I train you girls to be strong, focused, and proud of who you are. To stand up for yourselves. I train you to box so you won't ever *have* to fight. That may not make sense now, but—"

"Kitty, he was going to hurt my dog! What was I supposed to do? Say, 'Please, Mister Evil Guy, don't hurt my sweet little dog'?"

Kitty snorted. "A *dog*? You broke a guy's nose and put yourself in jeopardy over a *dog*?"

For the first time ever, I hated Kitty.

"Yes, Kitty," I said in a low voice. "In case you haven't heard, I'm a total fuckup. A loser. My boyfriend dumped me, I lost what few friends I have, and I'm on probation. But that 'dog' doesn't care that I'm a loser. My dogs are the only real friends I have."

She looked away. I tossed the hand wrapping on the floor. "What the hell kind of person would I be if I didn't stand up for my best friend, Kitty?"

She didn't answer. I headed for the locker room. Halfway across the training room, I turned and said, "Suspend me until the end of time if you want to. I don't care."

I sat on the bench in the locker room, once again staring at that amazing boxer in the poster. I hated myself for crying, but I couldn't help it. "I bet you never cry," I said to the woman who glared down at me from the wall. Christ. I *had* to be here. I *had* to train. What was I going to do?

I felt a hand on my shoulder. I looked up. It was Kitty. "Can I sit down?" she asked. I slid over to make room on the bench.

She took my bruised left hand in her strong black one, ran her thumb over the swollen knuckles. "Hurts like hell to hit something without those big ol' gloves on, doesn't it?"

"Yeah, it does."

She set my hand back in my lap. "Mardie, the reason I'm so strict about this is because of something that happened when I first started training girls to fight back in Philadelphia.

"I had this one girl, Bethany was her name. She'd had about every kind of abuse you could imagine in her fifteen years, so you couldn't blame her, but she was angry. And dangerous. I had to watch her like a hawk when she was sparring with one of the other girls. She was always on the edge of losing control."

I knew how that felt.

"Anyway," Kitty continued. "She started getting into fights outside of training. Stupid little fights at first—someone hassled her little sister, another kid stole her lunch money, that sort of thing. Then it seemed like she was fighting for no reason. Just itching to fight 'cause someone looked at her wrong. She'd come to training beat all to hell. Worried me to death. I should have suspended her from training, gotten her some help, but I didn't."

"Why not?" I asked. "You're pretty eager to suspend me."

Kitty rubbed her eyes like she was trying to scrub away a nightmare. "I was scared, Mardie. I thought I knew what I was doing, training these girls to fight. Heck, a couple of them ended up turning pro. But with her, I was in over my head. And I was too proud to admit it. So I just kept lecturing her, telling her not to fight, telling her to use her head rather than her fists."

"Did she?" I asked. I had a sinking feeling she didn't.

Kitty shook her head. "She picked a fight with the wrong guy. Great big, mean guy who hated women. Especially smart-mouthed women who wouldn't back down."

"What happened?"

Kitty's face went hard. "He killed her. Didn't matter how good a fighter she was, he had a gun and she didn't. That's all it came down to." Kitty stood up, rubbing her arms. "I swore if I ever trained girls to box again, I would never let them fight where I couldn't see them. I'd train them to use their heads rather than putting their bodies at risk."

I felt small up against Kitty's pain.

"I'm sorry, Kitty," I said.

Finally, she smiled at me. "Tell you what, you're suspended from the ring until January fifteenth."

I started to protest.

She held up her hand. "But you can still come and work out. No sparring, though. If you haven't busted any more faces, I'll let you back in the ring after that. Until then, you got to be on good behavior. Deal?"

"Deal," I said.

Kitty stood, then jerked her thumb at the woman in the poster. "I fought her once. Probably learned more in that one match than all the others put together."

"Who is she?" I asked.

"That's Laila Ali, girl. The King's daughter."

I gazed up at that fierce woman's face. "Wow, for real? Mohammed Ali's daughter?"

"Yes," Kitty replied. "And you can bet he would've come down on her like thunder if she'd ever busted some guy's nose."

TWELVE

It's a long flight from Denver to Atlanta. Amy and Dad sat in the seats behind Michael and me, playing cards. Michael had his headphones on listening to a book on CD. He'd let me have the window seat. He'd been pretty nice to me ever since I broke Eric's nose.

I leaned my head against the cool window. We were flying over Kansas. Flat Kansas, with its patchwork of farms and fields. I hadn't been out of the mountains in a long time.

I thought about this past week before we left. The little Christmas party over at Kitty's had been fun. She'd cooked what she said her family always ate on Christmas Eve: ham biscuits, scalloped potatoes, three-bean salad. It was good, but it was also funny to see Kitty in an apron. I'd never pictured her doing things like that. I know it sounds stupid, but I'd never really thought of her having a family before.

"How many brothers and sisters do you have?" I asked, as I helped her set the table. I'd gotten there before Shireen and Destiny.

"Just me," she said. "I was a late child. My folks didn't think they could have children, so I was a surprise."

"Did you grow up in Philadelphia?" I asked, remembering her story about the girl she trained there.

"Nope. Boston."

She pulled a bubbling dish of potatoes from the oven. "My dad was an accountant at a big firm there," she said. "My mom was a teacher."

My surprise must have shown. She laughed and said, "What? You think just because I'm black my family lived in the projects or something?"

"I'm sorry," I stammered. "It's just . . ."

She lit a cluster of white and red candles on the fireplace mantle. "I grew up in an almost all-white neighborhood and went to an almost all-white private school. I didn't really have a chance to be black until I went into the Air Force."

My jaw dropped. "The Air Force?"

Before I had a chance to ask her how the heck she ended up flying airplanes, the doorbell rang.

We sat around the living room, each of us groaning from too much food. Turned out Kitty was a good cook.

Kitty looked at us. "Okay, ladies, let's get down to business. It's no secret the three of you are my most talented boxers. And I'm itching to have winners in this year's Rocky Mountain Women's Golden Gloves Championship. Mardie and Shireen, since you're both under sixteen, you'll be in the junior division."

Shireen grinned and punched me on the thigh.

I realized I had no idea how old Destiny was. "Destiny too?"

"Nope, Destiny's nineteen. She'll be in the women's division."

Destiny said in her usual no-nonsense way, "When and where?"

"Denver, in June," Kitty said. "Which sounds a long time off, but it's not. We got a lot of work to do to get ready. It'll mean extra training sessions, more weight training, a lot more sparring, and matches with some other boxing clubs. It's a two-day tournament, which will mean a time commitment as well."

Kitty leaned forward. She placed her glass on the table. She looked at us intently. "If we're going to do this thing, it's going to require a lot of commitment from you three. Like I said, you have the talent, but that's not going to be enough. You're going to need focus and hunger."

Shireen laughed and patted her belly. "You know I always got room for more."

Kitty didn't laugh, though. "I'm serious, girls. You got to be hungry for this. You got to not just want it. You got to *believe* it. There are going to be at least twenty other girls who want this as bad as you do. No sense in me wasting my time or yours if you don't."

She looked at me. "I don't want to work with someone who's going to back out when training interferes with her social life or it gets too hard."

That stung, but I didn't say anything. Guess I had it coming.

She continued, "Suze can give me that commitment,

but she doesn't have the talent you guys do. But I need to know now. Are you hungry? Are you in?"

I thought about Eric and Ben and Megan and all the others who thought I was a loser, my father who thought I was a fuckup.

I nodded. "I'm in," I said. "I'll do it."

"Me, too," Shireen said. "Ain't nothin' gonna stop *la chica loca*." Kitty rolled her eyes.

"Destiny?" Kitty asked.

Destiny nodded.

Kitty raised her glass and said with a huge smile, "To us, then."

We clinked glasses, the crystal ringing. Shireen laughed. "They won't know what hit when 'Kitty's girls' show up in the ring."

Amy had arrived at that point to pick me up. "Sorry to break up the party, ladies," she said. "But we've got an early flight tomorrow and Mardie still has packing to do."

"I gotta go, too," Shireen said, as her mom's car pulled up by the curb. She gave me a quick hug. "*Feliz Navidad, chica*," she said. I was going to miss her.

Destiny pulled on her jacket. It looked like something she'd found in a Dumpster. Suddenly, I wondered what she was doing for Christmas.

Kitty waved us down the steps to the driveway. Snowing again. "You have a safe time and be ready to kick it up to high gear when you get back."

I remembered watching her standing in the porch light, snow drifting down around her. She got smaller and smaller as we drove away. But it was true, too, that she was somehow bigger to me after that night. I leaned my head back against the headrest.

"Have a good time?" Amy asked.

I smiled in the dark car. Someone sang "Have Yourself a Merry Little Christmas" on the radio.

"Yeah," I said. Remembering hearing Kitty say to Destiny, "I'll pick you up for Christmas Eve Mass," I said, "People sure are full of surprises."

Lynn and Jan's place in Georgia is about eight miles out from town on long, winding dirt roads. Perfect for running. I told myself, "Just try it once and see how it is." And it wasn't bad at all. Of course, as Dad pointed out, there's a big difference between running at almost sea level and running at forty-five hundred feet. But still, I had to admit it felt good. I didn't even mind when Dad went with me a couple of times. We didn't talk much, but that was okay. It was kind of nice. And Dad set a good pace. We'd run through the oaks and pine trees, just the sound of our breath and our footfalls. Destiny would have been proud.

We'd run back up the long hill, through the pastures to the old farmhouse, with its big porches. Michael and Amy would just be getting up. Lynn and Jan were usually out at the barn, taking care of the horses and checking their beehives.

Dad put his arm around my shoulder. "Good run, Mardie. You keep this up and we'll need to get you some real running shoes when we get home."

After breakfast, Michael usually went with Jan to her clinic. She's a vet and has a busy practice. For some reason, Michael liked going with her. She's kind of quiet and serious, like him.

Dad spent several hours in the morning on his laptop. Amy wasn't real happy about him bringing work to do. But he's coming up for tenure this year at the college. "Publish or perish," he says. Besides, there's talk of him becoming head of the history department.

So Amy and Lynn and I would pull on our jeans and saddle up the horses for a long ride. Amy was like a different person there. She and Lynn teased each other about old boyfriends and times they had gotten in trouble. They showed me where they'd built their own tree forts, favorite hiding places. They raced each other across the back pastures. I hadn't realized what a good rider Amy is. "Daddy put me up on a horse before I could walk," she said.

Lynn laughed. "And you put me up before I could walk."

"What about your mother?" I asked. "Did she teach you to ride, too?"

Lynn and Amy exchanged a look. Lynn said, "Mama didn't ride. She didn't like horses. Or dogs. Or living on this farm."

Amy looked sad. "She was a pretty unhappy person, honey."

Lynn said in a hard voice, "Nothing that a full bottle couldn't fix."

The night after Christmas, I was upstairs in the den watching an old movie on TV. I came downstairs to get something to drink. They all sat around the big wooden table in the kitchen talking.

It was serious talking, I could tell right away. Dad and Michael looked tense, and like they wanted to be anywhere else but there.

I got my glass of water and hurried back upstairs.

Later, as I got ready for bed, I heard low voices on the back porch. I looked out my window and saw Dad and Michael sitting on the porch steps. I was about to turn away, when Michael jumped up and paced back and forth on the porch. He said, "I don't know, Dad. I just *am*." My heart froze.

Dad put his head in his hands, the full moon shining on the back of his head. Michael sat down next to him.

I held my breath.

Dad sat up, put his arm around Michael's shoulders, and hugged him close. He murmured something I couldn't hear, but judging by how they sat there, I figured everything was going to be okay.

I was thinking hard about that night on our last day. Just Lynn and I were riding that morning. Amy and Dad had gone into town to visit an old friend of Amy's; Michael was with Jan, as usual.

Lynn pulled her horse up. "Let's walk a bit," she said. We tied the horses to a low branch. We'd ridden hard. They were just as happy to graze for a little while.

Lynn and I walked through an old field where their father used to grow tobacco. Lynn kicked at the old furrows with her boots. "Daddy used to find lots of arrowheads and spear points out here when he'd plow in the spring and fall. Might still be a few left."

We walked along in easy silence. Crows followed overhead, and Lynn's three Labrador retrievers trailed behind.

Finally I worked up the courage and said, "Michael's gay." I expected the earth to open up and swallow me or for Lynn to say, "Oh, Mardie, you're making things up."

Instead, she nodded and said, "Yes, I know."

I took a deep breath. Might as well dive in. "I outted him just before Thanksgiving to Dad and Amy. He was really mad at me."

Lynn squatted down and sifted dirt through her fingers. "Well, that probably wasn't the best way to do it. But it was good to get it out in the open anyway."

"Is that what everyone was talking about last night in the kitchen?"

"Yep," she said. "Amy said it was time. We had to practically drag your dad and Michael into the kitchen and force them to sit down to talk."

Lynn tossed a stick for the dogs. "Amy thought it would be easier with us."

"Why?" I asked.

"Because Jan and I are gay."

I stopped dead in my tracks. "You're gay?"

Lynn gave me a funny look. "Yeah. We both are. I thought you knew that."

I was stunned. Was everybody secretly gay?

I shook my head. "Why would I know that? It's not like I go around thinking about adults even having sex, straight or otherwise." It was too creepy to think about.

Lynn laughed. "True enough."

Before we knew it, it was time to head back to Colorado. Amy was sad to leave. She and Lynn hugged and hugged each other. Jan said something to Michael about staying in touch, which was kind of weird.

I shifted uncomfortably in my tiny airplane seat. Cowboys must have had calluses on their butts. I looked down at the clouds floating beneath the airplane.

Flying was cool. I adjusted the volume on my new iPod Michael gave me for Christmas with some of his favorite songs on it. Some of them were pretty weird and took some getting used to, but they were growing on me.

I nudged Michael and pointed out the window. He leaned across me and looked, then smiled. The snow-covered Rockies rose from the edge of the flat Kansas plain.

"Not long now," he said.

I gazed as far beyond the horizon as I could. I closed my eyes and imagined rising up and over the mountains, swooping down the other side to our little town. I saw the high school, the New Horizons Center, the library. The cemetery. I saw Alexis talking on the phone with Sam in her bedroom; Rick and Lizzie laughing as they watched Lizzie's favorite cartoons. The thought of Rick made my heart glad. Hannah and Feather circling the ring, Pete's steady hand always there; Kitty, Destiny, and Shireen training in the gym.

We were going home.

THIRTEEN

I ran every day after school, rain or shine. Just me, the dogs, and whatever route we took that day. If we hadn't had any snow that week, I ran the trails that wound up through the sage and scrub oaks. Sometimes we startled deer or elk bedded down in a ravine. If we'd had snow, I'd run the back streets through the old neighborhoods, up to the old silver mine, then down past the cemetery. Once or twice, I thought about going in and finding my mother's grave. But I couldn't seem to do it.

Sometimes I ran with Shireen if she wasn't babysitting her little brother and sister. When she did run with me, she talked nonstop. Even though she made me laugh, I missed the quiet of running alone. Every now and then, Michael joined me for a run. Michael was different lately, though. He wasn't mad at me anymore, but he didn't talk like he used to. He seemed to be a million miles away.

And then there was Dad. At first he wanted to run with me all the time. He even bought me a really cool pair of running shoes. But that was before the Phone Conversation.

It was a couple days after New Year's. I'd caught a ride

home from the gym with Shireen and her mom because Amy was in bed with the flu. I walked down the hall to Dad's study to ask him a question. I don't even remember about what, now.

As I started to push the door open, I heard Dad say, "Yeah, we had a great time in Georgia. I think it was really good for all of us to get away and do something together as a family." I could tell by his voice that Dad was talking to Pops, my grandfather.

"Michael's good," Dad said, although I noticed a little catch in his voice. "He's having a hard time deciding what schools to apply to. Don't quite know why he's dragging his feet all of a sudden, but I've got to get on him about it.

"Mardie's doing better. Her grades are up and she's not as moody as she was. Seems more focused. She's working out at the gym and running."

There was a pause, then a little laugh. "Oh, Amy told you about the boxing, huh? Who knows what that's all about. I think it's just a way to be different from everybody else, like dyeing her hair black. I doubt she'll stick with it."

I felt like Shireen had punched me in the stomach. Just "something to do"? Just "to be different"? Why was it that he took Michael's lacrosse so damn seriously but my boxing was a joke?

I'd had enough. I stalked into the study and planted myself right in front of Dad. The look on his face told me he'd never intended for me to hear that conversation. Too damn bad.

I held out my hand for the phone. "Oh hey, Dad, Mardie just came in and wants to talk to you. Here she is." He wouldn't even look when he handed me the phone.

Gripping the phone in my hand and looking directly at Dad, I said in an overly bright voice, "Hi, Pops! Happy New Year! Thanks for the Christmas check. I'm going to buy my own pair of boxing gloves with it! I want my own gloves because, despite what Dad may think, I *am* serious about boxing. Not only am I serious about boxing, I'm damned *good*. But Dad wouldn't know that because he's *never* bothered to come and watch me. And *I AM NOT A QUITTER!*"

I thrust the phone back at my father, walked out, and slammed the door to the study, then stomped up to my room. I locked the door and threw myself on the bed. For the first time in a long time, I wanted a cigarette or a joint— or to put my fist through the wall.

Instead, I did fifty pushups, and shitload of crunches.

I'd show him. I'd win that championship just to spite him, to prove him wrong.

A hesitant tap on my door. "Mardie, can I come in?"

Anger surged through me. "Go away, Dad." I could picture him rubbing the back of his neck, something he always does when he doesn't know what to say.

"Can I just come in for a minute?" he said.

My eyes felt dangerously wet and hot. "I'm not kidding, Dad. *Go away!*"

Before I had to hear his voice again, I put my headphones on and cranked up my iPod.

I took a deep breath and squeezed my eyes shut. I allowed one tear to slide down my cheek. But then resolve took over. No matter what Dad or anyone else thought, I would win. I needed to win. If it meant running ten miles a day, I'd run ten. If it meant training seven days a week, that's what I'd do. If it meant having no life, no friends outside the gym, well actually, that was typical for me now most of the time anyway. But still, it would be worth it to see the looks on all their faces—Dad, Ben, Eric, Megan, even Alexis—when I won the championship. Then I'd look down on all of them, knowing I hadn't needed any of them to get there. It would be perfect.

That need to win took my training to a whole new level.

Kitty watched me from one corner of the ring while Destiny watched Shireen from her corner. Sweat stung my eyes; our breathing was heavy and rhythmic.

Shireen threw a jab/hook combination but I ducked and caught her in the stomach. She gasped; her eyes widened in surprise, fear, and then anger. She swung wildly to the left, leaving her side unprotected. I moved in, nailing her just under the ribs. She staggered back.

"Gloves up, Shireen," Destiny called. Too late. I caught her with a hard straight right to the chin. One leg buckled. Destiny was right: running had made a huge difference. Just as I was about to move in, Kitty called time. "Go to your corners, ladies."

I sat on the stool and spit out my mouthpiece. Kitty squirted water in my mouth. "You're a different girl up there these days, Mardie. You look great. But don't forget who you're fighting. Don't let ego replace experience."

I watched Destiny talking close in Shireen's ear. Shireen nodded ever so slightly. I smiled as Kitty slipped the mouthpiece back in. This round was mine.

I strode to the center of the ring. We touched gloves. "Mix it up, ladies," Kitty called.

I bounced toward Shireen, moving lightly on the balls of my feet. *Should I play with her a little bit or finish her off?* I wondered. But before I could decide, a sledgehammer pounded into the side of my head, another just under my eye. Lights exploded. My mouthpiece flew across the canvas. I slammed into the floor.

I closed my eyes to stop the room from spinning. When I opened them again, three worried faces hovered over me.

Destiny unbuckled the chinstrap on my helmet. Kitty held three fingers up. "How many fingers, Mardie?" she asked. Just like in the movies.

Shireen clutched my hand, tears spilling down her cheeks. "I'm so sorry, *chica*. I never meant to hurt you, but you really pissed me off."

I worked my jaw back and forth and gently touched the area just under my eye. It was already swelling. The amazing thing was, it didn't hurt. I had just taken the worst hit ever, and it didn't even hurt. Cool.

I admired my face in the mirror the next morning. The most amazing shades of purple, yellow, and green reflected back at me. I touched the purplest part, just under my eye. Not too bad. Still, I did my best to cover it up with makeup. I knew the Professor would not be keen on the new look.

He was at the stove when I went into the kitchen. He flipped a pancake in the skillet. "Morning, bug," he said.

I tried my best to keep my face turned away from him. "Morning, Dad," I said.

Michael came into the kitchen. He whistled. "Good-lookin' shiner, sis." *Crap*.

"Shiner?" Dad turned around and his mouth dropped open. He face went from white to red.

"What the heck happened to you, Mardie?"

Guess my makeup didn't do such a great job. "I forgot who I was boxing last night, that's all."

Dad stepped over to take a closer look. He winced like he'd been the one popped in the face. "I don't like the looks of that. Maybe we should take you to the doctor."

"It looks a lot worse than it feels, Dad. It really doesn't hurt, and it didn't hurt at all when it happened. It was actually kind of cool. Kitty says—"

"Getting a black eye is not 'cool,' " Dad snapped. "What are people going to think when you walk into school with a black eye?"

"I don't care what other people think," I said.

"Well, *I do*, Mardie."

"Why, Dad? Why do you care? Are you afraid people will think *you* hit me? Are you afraid people will think they're dark secrets at Professor Wolfe's house?"

"No, Mardie, I don't want people thinking I don't take care of you. You're my daughter, for god's sake."

We stared at each other for a moment. He took a deep breath and said, "I'm not sure I want you boxing anymore."

I was just about to tell Dad where he could stick his parental authority when Amy wandered in. She handed him a cup of coffee.

"May I remind you that Michael lost two back teeth and broke his thumb twice playing lacrosse?" she said.

"That's different," Dad said.

"How?" Amy and I asked in unison.

"Look, I agreed to this boxing thing *as long as she didn't get hurt*. I believe those were my exact words, were they not?"

"It doesn't hurt, Dad," I said. "It just looks bad. Besides, you also said I could box as long as I kept my grades up. I've done that. I've got all As and Bs this quarter, I've stayed out of trouble. I've kept my end of the bargain."

Dad rubbed the back of his neck.

"They wear helmets, gloves, and mouth guards, Dave. The trainer always watches everything they do." In a lower voice, Amy said, "And you'd know that if you came and watched her train."

Dad looked at us, shook his head, and left without a word.

At training Thursday night, Kitty said, "Okay, you two. What did you learn from your last encounter in the ring?"

Shireen said, "I learned white girls can hit."

I said, "I learned that it doesn't hurt much when you get hit really hard."

Kitty sighed and shook her head. She waved Destiny over. "Destiny, what *should* these two smart-asses have learned from their little bout in the ring Tuesday night?"

Destiny said in her usual succinct way, "Emotions can screw you up."

Shireen and I looked at each other, then at Kitty.

"She's right," Kitty said. "Shireen, what did you say when you told Mardie why you hit her so hard the other night?"

Shireen bit her lip in concentration, then said, "I told her I hit her so hard because she pissed me off?"

Kitty nodded. Then she turned to me. "And what were you feeling just before you got knocked on your ass?"

That wasn't hard to remember. "I was going to win the match without any problem."

"And what did I say to you before you went back into the ring?"

That took a little more thought. I shrugged. "Sorry, I can't remember."

Kitty frowned. "*Or* you weren't listening. And you weren't listening for the same reason you got your little white butt knocked to the floor: *hubris*."

"Hugh who?" Shireen asked.

"*Hubris*," Destiny said. "It's a Latin word that means you got too much pride."

"Or as my mama would say, you got a big head," Kitty said. "Either way, you both brought emotions—anger and ego—into the ring that don't belong there. Any boxer worth his or her salt will tell you that emotions like anger, re-

134

venge, swelled-up pride will do you a lot more harm than good when you come up against an opponent. Those emotions rob you of your focus, and your focus is your power."

"But," Shireen protested, "it was because I was so angry that I was able to win the match."

"Yes, but your anger and your *fear* almost lost you the match before I called time, didn't it? And Mardie, your big head caused you to do what?"

Remembering now what she'd said to me as I sat on that stool, glorying in what a great boxer I'd become, I said, "It caused me to forget who I was fighting. I just thought about the fact that I was winning. I lost my focus."

Kitty finally smiled. "Your best weapon in the ring is self-control. You both have improved a lot, physically and in terms of technique over the last couple of months. But you got to master your *emotions* if you're going to win. It's the difference between boxing and fighting."

There's a difference? That's something I'd never thought about.

In the locker room, I watched Shireen (talking a mile a minute to herself in the mirror) change into her usual camo cargo pants and hoodie. She ran her fingers through her short, sleek hair while I undid my sweaty braid. Most of the Latino girls had long, Jennifer Lopez–type hair. But not Shireen.

"Who cuts your hair?" I asked.

"I do," she said.

"You cut your own hair?"

"Yeah," she said, turning back to the mirror. "It's not hard and it's a lot cheaper than going to someone."

I stood next to her, studied my own reflection in the mirror. I raked my fingers through the long tangle of hair I'd had my whole life.

"Cut mine," I said.

"Right."

"I'm serious," I said. "I'm sick of it. It's a pain."

"Guess I could," she said. "When?"

"Sooner the better," I said. "Tomorrow."

She zipped up her bag. "Okay. But you'll need to come over to my house. I got to watch the sibs after school."

"No problem," I said.

I took the bus home with Shireen after school the next day. Most of the kids on the bus were Latino. I felt entirely too white and too tall. I was relieved when Shireen nudged me and said, "We get off here."

I'd never been in Shireen's house. It was small and crammed full of stuff: toys, books, magazines, and every color pillow you could imagine. The walls were covered with photographs.

A small woman pushed herself off the couch, dislodging one of several cats.

Shireen bent down and kissed her cheek, saying something to her in Spanish.

"Mardie, this is my grandmother."

I searched my brain for what pitiful little bits of Spanish I knew. *"Buenos dias,"* I said. *"Como estas?"*

She beamed and nodded. "*Muy bien*, Mardie. *E usted?*"

"Uh . . ." I looked at Shireen for help.

"She said, 'Very good, Mardie. And you?'"

I smiled and nodded back. "*Muy bien.*"

The front door banged open. Shireen's little brother wiped his feet on the mat and dropped his backpack by the door.

"A.J., this is my friend, Mardie."

A.J. turned. Military dog tags hung from a chain around his neck. He glanced at me shyly. "Hi," he said, then ducked into the kitchen.

Shireen shrugged. "A man of few words," she said.

Just then the most amazing sight paraded into the living room: a smaller version of Shireen in a pink ballet tutu, tights in red, yellow, purple, and green stripes, a Winnie the Pooh sweatshirt, and a silver feather boa, all teetering on top of black high heels five sizes too big. I was stunned at the sight. Shireen's grandmother laughed.

Shireen sighed. "Tiffany, how many times I told you to stay out of Mama's makeup?"

I hadn't even noticed the makeup, which was truly amazing, too.

"I have to practice," she said in a little Minnie Mouse voice. "I have a very important party this weekend." I laughed.

"And just how important can a party for six-year-olds be?" Shireen asked.

Studying the four-foot vision in front of me, I said, "Very."

Shireen's grandmother pulled on her coat and scarf. "See you tomorrow, *Abuela*," Shireen said, hugging her goodbye.

Then she turned to me and said, "You ready?"

It's amazing we all fit in the tiny kitchen, but we did. I sat on a stool, head in the kitchen sink, the little beauty queen on a hot pink pillow on the floor. A.J. pretended not to watch from the table in a corner.

Shireen's fingers massaging the shampoo into my hair felt amazing. "I might hire you to do this on a regular basis," I sighed.

"Mmmm . . . ," Shireen said. "I know what you mean. When Grandma washes my hair, I practically fall asleep."

She wrung water from my hair, then sat me up. Wrapping a towel around my head, she said, "Now we go to my room for the mirror."

I don't know what I was expecting Shireen's room to look like, but whatever I expected, it was not what I saw when she swung open the door. Unlike the chaos and clutter of the rest of the house, Shireen's room was spare and clean. It held only a bed, a row of bookshelves made of wood and cinder block, a low chest of drawers, and a large round mirror over the chest of drawers. That was it. Except pinned to the white walls were dozens of pen-and-ink drawings. I stepped closer to look. At first glance, the drawings were random, abstract. But the more you looked, the more you saw the connections between recognizable, everyday objects. The logic of the connections told a story. And some of the stories were disturbing.

"Wow," I said stepping back. "Where did you get these? They're amazing."

For the first time ever, I saw Shireen blush.

Princess Tiffany twirled and said, "My big sister is a *great* artist!"

I shook my head. "These are awesome!"

I sat on the stool Shireen brought from the kitchen, a towel draped over my shoulders. Looking around the room again as Shireen teased the tangles from my hair, I asked, "So how did you get into boxing?"

"When Papa got deployed the first time, I kind of freaked. I couldn't handle it. So I started running with a bad crowd, getting into all kinds of trouble. We lived in the city, then, so there was lots of trouble to get into. Even went to juvie for a while."

I watched her face in the mirror. It was calm, showed no emotion.

"My mom got the job at Summit Hospital, so we moved here. She figured in little South Eden, there wasn't much trouble I could find. One day I was going through the newspaper, and right there in the sports section was an interview with Kitty. I read the article. It was all about how good boxing is for teenage girls, especially ones getting into trouble and stuff. For some reason, I knew it was something I needed."

She ran the comb from the top of my head down to the middle of my back in one long stroke. "So when Mama came home that night, I showed her the article and told her I wanted to sign up."

Remembering my dad's reaction, I said, "I bet she didn't go for that."

Shireen laughed. "Actually, I was so out of control, I think she would have tried anything."

"She was a *bad, bad* girl," Tiffany said from Shireen's bed. We both laughed.

"Too true, little mouse," Shireen said.

She combed the last of the tangles from my hair. "That was over a year ago, and I'm still there."

"Why?" I asked.

Shireen chewed her bottom lip. "I don't have to pretend how I feel when I'm there." Glancing over at her little sister, she said, "It's hard, with Papa gone. We never know day to day. . . . So I try to be happy all the time for Mama's sake, you know?"

I nodded.

"But there, especially in the ring, I can be angry and scared and pissy if I feel like it and no one cares. No one tells me I should feel this or I shouldn't feel that."

"So where does *la chica loca* come from?"

"Like I said, when we lived in the city, I ran with some bad kids. I guess it was like a gang. And they were always getting into it with other gangs." She took a deep breath, her hands resting on my shoulders. "One day, some kids from another gang cornered me after school. They teased me about being fat, about my dad being black." We locked gazes in the mirror, then she looked away. "They said terrible things about my family. And then they beat the snot out of me."

"Wow," I breathed. "What did you do?"

"Not a damn thing," she said. "I didn't fight back, didn't even try to defend myself. I was too scared. It was humiliating."

She smiled but her eyes were hard. "*La chica loca* comes from that humiliation. She's my stronger half, now. When I'm up in the ring, I suck up all that fear and humiliation and unleash the heat."

I nodded. "That explains a lot."

"Now," she said, flashing the pair of scissors. "What about this hair?"

"Cut it," I said. "Cut it all off."

I closed my eyes. I felt the scissors moving slowly across the top of my shoulders. With every snip, I felt lighter.

"There," she said.

I opened my eyes. My hair brushed the tops of my shoulders. I swung my head back and forth. The hair swung with it.

"More," I said. "I want it *off*. I want it totally different."

"I don't know, *chica*," she said. "Maybe you should try this out first. It's a big change."

I held out my hand, watching her face in the mirror. "Give me the scissors, then."

She started to say something. Our eyes locked in the mirror—just like they had so many times in the ring. She handed me the comb and scissors. I grabbed a fistful of hair, took a deep breath and cut. There was no turning back. With every clump of hair that fell to the floor, I felt like another layer of the old me was falling away, too.

"Wow," Shireen breathed.

I had to agree. The long hair I'd hid behind all my life was gone. Looking back at me in the mirror was a face of details I'd never noticed before. Sharp cheekbones, big eyes, a pointed chin, eyebrows that tilted up. And best of all, my nose looked smaller.

Shireen squirted a little gel in her palm and tousled my hair. Then she took her fingers and scrunched. Curls! I actually had curls! Nothing like Michael or my mother, but just enough to be interesting.

Shireen pinched the tips of my ears. "Look at those," she said. "They look like little elf ears. So cute!"

I turned my head this way and that. I'd never noticed what a long neck I had. It was kind of pretty. I smiled at myself in the mirror. "Dad's going to freak," I said.

This wasn't his little bug looking out of the mirror now. I felt ten times lighter.

"I just cannot get over how different you look," Amy said as we drove across town, home.

"You think Dad's going to freak?" I asked.

She laughed. "Oh, yeah."

"Why?" I asked. "It's just hair."

"It's not about the hair, Mardie. It's about you changing. About you not being his little girl anymore."

"But everything changes," I said, thinking about Michael, thinking about my life.

Amy sighed. "That's what I keep telling your father."

"Dad's pretty oblivious," I said. "Maybe he won't notice."

We walked in the front door. Dad was in the kitchen taking something out of the oven.

I thought about escaping to my room before he could see me. But then I figured I might as well get it over with.

I walked to the breakfast bar, sat down. "Smells good, Dad."

He turned around, smiling. "It's—"

And just like in the movies, his eyes went wide and he dropped the loaf of banana bread onto the floor. "Mardie Marie Wolfe," he gasped. "What have you done?"

Amy came up behind me, ran her fingers through my hair. "I think it's cute. She looks like a little baby bird."

I groaned.

Dad just stared. He didn't even yell at the dogs, having a field day eating the banana bread off the floor. Finally, he said, "But your hair, Mardie. It was so pretty. You've always worn it long."

I shrugged. "I was tired of it, Dad. I needed a change."

"Yeah, but—"

"It's just hair," I told him. "It's not that big a deal."

He stooped to clean up the banana bread off the floor. The dogs hadn't left much. "I don't know how much more change I can take around here," he muttered.

Saturday at New Horizons was busy, but weird. We'd had a huge snowstorm the night before and it continued all the next morning. A lot of the volunteers didn't show that day, and several of my favorite people—Roger, Lizzie, Kaitlin, and even Hannah—were home sick. At least Rick was there, somewhere.

I'd just finished cleaning out the last stall when Pete leaned over the stable door and said, "I can't believe you came out in this weather, Mardie. I don't know what I would have done without you."

I wiped the sweat out of my eyes with the back of my hand, careful not to get horse poop on my face. "Didn't really have anything better to do. Besides, I thought today might be the day Hannah rode for twenty minutes."

Pete sighed and shook his head. "It always scares the hell out of me when that kid gets sick. Do me a favor and saddle up Granite over there," he said. "Take him through his paces in the ring. He needs a good workout."

I was honored. Pete had never let me just take one of the horses and ride before. And everyone knew Granite wasn't the easiest horse to handle.

"Just me and Granite?" I said.

Already on his way out of the barn, Pete said over his shoulder, "Relax, Mardie. I trust you."

I kept the lead on the big horse's halter fairly tight as I walked him from the stables to the indoor ring. A gust of wind blew snow across the floor. Granite's eyes grew big. He tossed his huge head and skittered sideways. "Easy, big guy," I said in a low voice. "It's just a little snow."

I eased him into a trot, then into a canter around the ring. He was wired up, nervous. I tried to take him through some figure eights and roundabouts. "Focus, buddy. Focus," I said. His emotions were getting the best of him.

I took him through the cones, weaving in and out. First at a fast walk, then a trot. In and out, once, twice. Then around the ring fast, and back to the center. Just like when it was me and Shireen up in the ring, or when I worked the speed bag, I felt completely me.

"Lookin' good."

I about jumped out of my skin. Granite skittered to one side. "Whoa boy," I said, patting his neck.

Rick sat on the top rail of the fence. He smiled. "I didn't know you could ride so well."

I walked Granite over to Rick. "I am a woman of many talents," I said.

"No doubt," Rick said, laughing. "Want to go out some time and tell me about all those talents?"

FOURTEEN

On Monday, for the first time in forever, Alexis actually ate lunch with me. Guess I was her fallback when her other friends weren't around.

I felt a little pissy. I mean, she'd blown me off so many times. But a friend is a friend. Besides, I needed to talk to her about Rick.

"The thing is," I said to Alexis at lunch, "I get the distinct vibe he wants to ask me out."

Alexis shrugged. "So?"

"I've sworn *off* guys. Don't want anything to do with them."

"So don't go out with him. Tell him to sniff around somewhere else."

She didn't sound like Alexis. But then, Alexis and I hadn't exactly been spending much time together lately.

"Well, he's a nice guy, though. And we do work together at New Horizons every Saturday. I'd hate to lose him as a friend. But," I said, "I can't let anything interfere with training."

"I noticed," Alexis mumbled. "Is that why you cut your hair like that?"

I grinned, running my fingers through my spikes and curls. "You like it?"

Alexis rolled her eyes.

"And what's with you, still going to that place all day on Saturdays anyway? I thought you were done with your community service by now."

It was true. I'd finished my one hundred hours of court-ordered time last month. Even Judge Martinez was surprised I was still going on my own. I told her (this time without Dad and Amy) that I liked being there, and felt that maybe I made a little bit of a difference. And as Rick said, I learned things from the people I used to think were "freaks."

"Gotten under my skin, I guess. I've made friends there."

"The handicapped and the Hispanic kids. That's just great, Mardie."

"What the hell's wrong with you? You didn't used to be so—"

Just then, Megan sauntered by our table. She "accidentally" kicked my backpack across the floor. It slid to a stop by the Jock Table.

"Oops," she said covering her mouth. "Clumsy me." Then she sneered, "You gonna break *my* nose now, dyke?"

Actually, I was amazed. Rather than feeling like the top of my head would explode if I didn't take her on, I just took some deep breaths and let my arms relax. I counted to ten (well, maybe six), stepped around her as if she were just a bug on the floor, and walked over to retrieve my stuff.

And who was holding it out to me, deadly grin on his face? Eric Lindstrom. "Come to papa," he said.

The cafeteria grew quiet. I heard Kitty's voice say, "It is always best to let the enemy defeat himself."

I let out a long, dramatic sigh. "Eric, Eric, Eric," I said. "Didn't you learn *anything* the last time we 'chatted'?"

He looked me up and down. "Yeah," he said with a snort. "I learned you're a freak, just like that fag brother of yours." Hoots from the other jocks, nervous twitters from the Cheerleader Table.

I smiled, taking one step forward. "And you want to know what I learned, Eric?"

"That a white girl can kick his ass," a voice from behind me said.

I glanced over my shoulder and there was every guy— and some of the girls—from the Latino tables, all standing behind me, backing me up.

Eric's eyes darted back and forth.

I shook my head and stepped right up to the King of the Jock Table's face. My posse took a step forward, too, and I felt ten feet taller.

"I learned that you are one scared asshole. You are so scared of anything that's different that you have to pick on girls and *defenseless* little *dogs*. That's just sad, dude. Really sad." Louder still, I said, "Hurting a little dog is just *sick*."

That did the trick. Just what I was hoping to hear: outraged mutterings from the group behind me and (most importantly) the Vegan Table. "He hurt a *defenseless animal*? A little *dog*?" The mutterings rose to a tidal roar. I turned around and walked slowly away, leaving Eric to the wolves.

Rick brought my backpack to English class. He handed it to me with a grin. And a note. The note said, "How about pizza and ice skating Friday night?"

I glanced over at him with a weak smile. What was I going to do? I could avoid him as much as possible. But that option felt pretty crappy. I could go out with him on Friday and miss training. That felt completely unacceptably crappy.

"Hey Rick," I called on the way out of class. He turned around and smiled.

I took a deep breath. "Here's the thing: I really like you as a friend but I'm just real over guys right now, and I don't know if I'll ever trust them again *ever*, and so all my energy is totally devoted to training for a boxing championship in June, which I *have* to win to show everybody, including my *Dad*, that I'm not a loser and I train on Friday nights so—"

Rick held up his hand. "Okay, okay! Geez, Mardie, I wasn't asking you to marry me and be the mother of my children. All I had in mind was doing something fun."

I looked down at the floor and cleared my throat. "Oh."

He reached out and touched my hand. In a lower voice he said, "I won't kid you, Mardie. I really like you. I think you're amazing."

"*Right*," I said.

"It's true. You're smart, funny, tough, and you've got a good heart."

"And how would you know anything about my heart?"

"Oh come on, Mardie. I see you every Saturday with Roger and Kaitlin, and especially Hannah."

I studied my shoes.

"Besides, my sister's crazy about you, and she's the best judge of character I know. But I don't want to interfere with your training. I think it's cool that you box. A little scary, but cool."

I laughed in spite of myself.

The bell rang. He looked away, shouldered his backpack. "Looks like we'll be late to class."

I put my hand on his arm. "I don't train Saturday night. How about then?"

Rick grinned. "Cool."

"But I have to warn you," I said. "I really suck at ice skating."

He laughed. "Great, because I'm actually damn good."

"By the way," he said, as we made our way down the hall. "I like the hair."

FIFTEEN

Friday night, Kitty said, "Gather 'round girls. I have some news." Shireen plopped down at Kitty's feet with a groan. I'd been hitting on all cylinders that night and kicked her ass. Plus, she hadn't been running because of the snow. A definite mistake.

"Okay. Remember I said that you girls were going to need to get some matches in before the championship in June?"

We nodded.

"Well, I've contacted as many amateur boxing clubs as I could find within a four-hour drive."

"How many did you find?" Shireen asked.

"Not as many as I'd hoped, about seven."

"And do they all have girl fighters?" I asked.

Kitty sighed. "No. That narrowed it down to about three. But," she said, brightening, "I know most all those trainers and they're good. They should have some girls that'll give us some decent matches."

"So when's the first match?" Shireen asked.

"In three weeks. On March twentieth, in Colorado Springs. It's a good, solid boxing club. You should each get a decent match. So," Kitty said, handing us each a form, "there are a couple of things you have to do to get your A.I.B.A. passbook. First, your parents have to sign this form saying you have their permission to compete."

"I'm screwed," I groaned.

"It's the law," Kitty said. "After that, you have to get this physical evaluation form filled out by your doctor saying you're of sound mind and body. Then you can get your passbook."

I chewed my lip. "Any way we can compete without a passbook?"

Kitty shook her head. "Those are the Amateur Boxing Association's rules. They use the passbook to match you up with fighters with similar experience and size. They also check it before every match to see if you have any doctor-ordered suspensions. Do you need me to talk to your folks? I thought they knew you were training for the championship."

"In theory, yes," I said. "But when Dad saw that shiner Shireen gave me a few weeks ago, he totally freaked. He almost made me quit boxing."

Kitty said, "Well, I'd be happy to talk to your dad if you want me to, Mardie. I've done it many times before. Dads tend to have the hardest time with the idea of their 'little girl' punching someone in the face. And getting hit."

"You're awful quiet tonight." Amy drove past the mall.

I watched the snow dance in the headlights. After a long minute I said, without much enthusiasm, "I have my first real match in three weeks. Over in Colorado Springs."

"Wow," Amy said, glancing over at me. "That's pretty exciting, isn't it?"

"It would be, except Dad has to sign a form saying I have his permission to fight. And I figure there's a snowball's chance in you-know-where that he'll do that."

Amy was quiet. Then she said, "I wish I could say to you that we'd bypass your dad and I would sign it instead, but that would be dishonest. And you know how I feel about dishonesty."

Would they *ever* let me forget the stupid things I'd done? "You couldn't sign it anyway," I snapped. "You're not my real mom."

Amy blanched like I'd slapped her in the face. I looked away.

She pulled into the driveway and turned off the car without opening the garage. We sat there in the quiet dark, snow falling all around.

"I'm sorry your mother died, Mardie. I'm sorry you never really had a chance to know her. I do have some idea what it's like to miss your mother." She continued quietly, "I know I'm not your and Michael's biological mother, but I don't know how a mother could be any more 'real' than I've been. Without giving birth to you, that is."

"Sorry," I said, looking down at my hands.

Amy pressed the remote on the garage door opener. We watched the door slowly rise, heard the dogs barking.

As she put the car in gear, Amy said, "We'll talk to your dad together. How about that?"

"Guess what?" Dad said, giving Amy a kiss and me a quick hug. He hadn't tried to hug me since our blowup just after Christmas.

"Your dad's coming for a visit?" Amy asked, as she wrestled Max for his stuffed pink octopus.

"How'd you know?" Dad asked. "Did he already tell you he's coming?"

Amy laughed at the expression on his face. She reached up and playfully tugged on his earlobe. "No, silly man. I *know* because first, nothing gets you this excited except your dad coming for a visit, and second, he always comes this time of year."

It was true. Pops lives in Arizona and, as he says, he "can only take that damned sunshine and all those widow women for just so long." Then he packs up his VW camper van, his cat Ratchet, and Bob the canary, and they hit the road. No matter where else they go, they always wind up here. Dad says Pops makes a point of coming in February to remind him of why he moved to a place where it never snows.

I hoped that maybe having Pops here would put Dad in a good enough mood to sign the consent form.

"So what's his ETA?" Amy called from the kitchen.

"Estimated time of arrival is not for a couple weeks," Dad said. "He's going to Mesa Verde first."

Damn. So much for that plan.

After I scarfed down a plate of leftover spaghetti, Amy raised her eyebrows and nodded toward Dad.

I plopped down next to him on the couch. He was engrossed in yet another of the seemingly endless World War II documentaries on TV. I sat there fidgeting with my shoelace, then cleared my throat.

Barely tearing his eyes away from yet another exploding tank, he said, "What is it, bug?"

"There's something I need you to sign, Dad."

"Something for school? Field trip?"

"Not exactly," I said.

He frowned. "Then what?"

I glanced at Amy, who was still in the kitchen. I thought she said we'd talk to him together.

I took a deep breath. "It's for boxing, that's all. No big deal." I held the form out to him. Maybe he wouldn't actually read it.

Wrong. He read it over, right down to the fine print. His frown deepened. "I don't know about this, Mardie."

My frustration rose as my heart sank. "It's just a match, Dad, and I have to have a certain number of them to qualify for the championship in June."

Dad started to say something when Amy came over and sat down. "Dave, it's just like when Michael's lacrosse team has to win a certain number of local games to go to the state finals."

"No, it's *not* 'just like' that, Amy. You keep comparing Mardie's boxing to Michael's lacrosse and it's not the same at all."

Dad's temple vein was pulsing again. This was hopeless.

But Amy was unfazed. "I know it's not the same, Dave. Because this is Mardie, your little girl, getting involved in a sport that's culturally unacceptable for women, and one you don't want your daughter to participate in." She had him there, and Dad knew it.

"I don't want my daughter to become a spectacle," Dad muttered.

Amy looked at me and waited.

"Times have changed, Dad. There are lots of girls and women training at boxing clubs. There's even an association that has all these rules about women boxing. Kitty says it might even be an official Olympic sport at the 2012 games."

"There you have it," Amy said, getting up from the couch. "That's good enough for me."

Dad glared at Amy. "Hold on. None of us knows anything about amateur boxing," Dad said. "Let's have Mardie's trainer explain to us exactly what happens."

Dad, the perennial professor.

Amy nodded. "Sounds reasonable. That way you'd be making an informed decision rather than an emotional one."

Dad was quiet. Then he said, "Mardie, if we meet with Kitty, will you abide by whatever decision I make about this and not argue with me?"

"As long as you listen to her with an open mind."

He held out his hand. I took it. He shook it once. "Deal?"

"Deal."

The Ring

Saturday night. I wiped the steam off the bathroom mirror after I got out of the shower. Running and boxing had definitely changed my body. I had muscles now you could actually see in my arms and shoulders. My legs were hard and strong.

At first I freaked when I started putting on weight. But Kitty convinced me that muscle weighs more than fat. So as I got stronger, I weighed more. I had to admit, for the first time ever, I even liked the way I looked.

Not that that did me a whole lot of good skating with Rick that night.

After I fell on my butt for the millionth time, Rick sat down on the ice next to me and said, "You're forcing it too much, Mardie. You can't muscle your way through skating. In skating, everything's soft and fluid."

"Right," I said.

Rick pulled me up by both hands, holding them just a few seconds longer than he needed to. Then he put one arm around my waist. His arm was surprisingly strong.

"Now," he said. "Mirror everything exactly the way I do it. Push off on the same leg. Switch legs when I do. And stay loose, okay? Ready?"

We pushed off and glided across the ice. At first I held myself stiffly, trying to set the pace.

"Just relax, Mardie," he said.

I took a deep breath and then I did.

I was nervous Tuesday night during training. Dad and Amy were coming to meet with Kitty afterward, to discuss my competing. I knew Amy would keep an open mind, but would Dad?

Fortunately, Shireen was in rare form that night when we sparred, forcing me to stay focused. She may not have been running, but she was definitely spending extra time in the weight room. When her gloved fist connected with any part of my body, I felt like I was on the receiving end of a jackhammer.

The bell rang. "Time," Kitty called from the apron corner. "Good work!" Shireen wrapped me in a sweaty hug. I cuffed her head. Spitting out the mouthpiece, I looked to the other corner and saw Amy and Dad. How long had they been watching?

Kitty followed my gaze. Smiling, she waved Dad and Amy over to ringside. "How're you doing? You got to see my two prize students mixing it up tonight!"

Amy grinned. "You looked great up there, Mardie. You both looked really strong." Shireen smiled and blushed. "Thanks, Mrs. Wolfe." I waited for Amy to do the last-name thing. Much to my amazement, she didn't.

I glanced nervously at Dad. He didn't say anything.

Kitty looked from Dad to me. "Why don't we all go to my office? I understand you have some questions about how these matches work." Dad looked at me and nodded.

I'd never been in Kitty's office before. It was surprisingly neat. One wall was covered with photos of girl fighters and formal-looking certificates. Others showed Kitty with arms raised triumphantly in the ring; Kitty in one of those military flight suits, a helmet tucked under one arm, her other hand resting on the flat gray side of a fighter jet. In another corner was a tall bookcase filled with trophies and books. Behind her desk was a bulletin board with training and class schedules written in a neat hand.

Dad, Amy, and I squeezed in together on a plaid love seat. Kitty sat behind her desk. Clasping her hands in front of her, she leaned forward. She looked my dad square in the eye. "You are very conflicted about Mardie boxing, aren't you, Mr. Wolfe?" she asked.

Dad nodded.

Kitty continued in a low, almost soothing voice. "You want to support Mardie. You want her to succeed. You've even seen how these past few months of training have helped her. And you just saw how talented she is in the ring."

"I *do* want Mardie to succeed. I'm just not sure about boxing. I mean, I don't even like to see men box, much less women. And certainly not my daughter."

Kitty leaned forward. "I don't blame you, Mr. Wolfe. I don't blame you at all. If I had a daughter, I sure as heck wouldn't want her doing what you see those professional male fighters doing up there in the ring. Pounding each other till they look like raw meat. It's disgusting. And dangerous."

Amy and I glanced at each other.

Kitty smiled sympathetically. She pushed a dish of Jelly Bellies toward Dad. "Have some jelly beans, Mr. Wolfe, and let me explain to you about amateur boxing."

Kitty pulled a stack of papers out of a drawer in her desk and brought them around to my dad. I glanced over at the sheets, which were all different colors. The yellow one was labeled HISTORY OF WOMEN'S BOXING. The green one was labeled RULES OF THE GAME. The pink one was labeled TEN IMPORTANT THINGS TO KNOW ABOUT AMATEUR BOXING. The Professor was impressed.

Kitty perched on top of her desk. "I won't take up your time this evening going into the history of women's boxing. But I hope you'll read that sheet. I think you'll be surprised to see how long women have been boxing." She glanced over at me. "I'd like you to read it, too, Mardie."

"The important thing for you to know is that amateur boxing is much less risky than professional boxing." Ticking off the points on her fingers, she went on. "First of all, amateur boxers have to wear protective headgear and mouthpieces. Women must also wear chest protectors. Secondly, the main objective in an amateur match is to score points, not knock out the other person. As a matter of fact, the point scoring isn't even based on the force of the blow."

"What's it based on then?" I asked. This was news to me.

"It's based on technique, finesse. Athletic talent. It's a lot like fencing that way."

"In other words," Amy said, "it's based more on brains than brawn, right?"

Kitty smiled. "Exactly. And that's what I train into these girls every minute of every session. Use your brains more than your fists. Right, Mardie?"

I nodded. "That's for sure."

"That's all well and good," Dad said. "But the fact remains, these girls are strong and they *are* hitting each other. I saw that for myself tonight. How do I know that in the heat of competition, things won't get out of hand and Mardie will get hurt?"

"Good question. One of the big differences, though, between amateur boxing and what you see at Caesars Palace in Las Vegas is how tightly controlled the match is by the referees. Trust me, they do *not* hesitate to stop a match or disqualify a fighter. If there's any blood flowing, like from a cut brow that can't be stopped, the fight is stopped. Immediately. And in women's matches, there are only three rounds, each two minutes long. With all the protective gear, the refs, and the short rounds, the risks are truly minimal."

Dad looked down at the brightly colored sheets and sighed. "I don't know. . . ."

Kitty placed her hand on his. "Mr. Wolfe, I won't lie to you. Yes, Mardie may get a black eye, or some bruised ribs. And you can probably tell this lovely beak of mine's seen some action. But Mardie's good. Really good. I don't know how she'll do out there competing, but I do know she's come a long way in the ring."

"Outside the ring, too," Amy said.

Dad looked at the sheets for what seemed like forever, then he looked at me. "You really want to do this, Mardie?"

I held my breath and nodded, not daring to speak.

"If I sign that form, Mardie, can you understand that even though I may give my consent, that doesn't mean I'm comfortable with it?"

An edge of disappointment speared my heart. "Guess I can't have everything," I said.

Kitty pulled a consent form from thin air. She placed it in front of Dad, clicking open a pen. As Dad read the form, Kitty said, "I promise you, Mr. Wolfe, I've trained Mardie to box as intelligently and safely as possible. And I'll make sure she carries that knowledge into the ring. I care a great deal for Mardie. And all my girls."

Taking the signed form from my dad's hand, she locked eyes with him and said, "Family support means a great deal to any athlete, but particularly these girls. They need to know it's okay to be different. To be who they are. Just the act of a girl taking up boxing requires a kind of bravery most athletes don't possess."

My cheeks flushed with pride. I glanced over at Dad. He couldn't meet my eyes.

I marked off the days before my first match with red Xs, took long runs, and spent extra time in the weight room. Amy got more excited with each passing day. She offered to drive all of us to Colorado Springs. "The van will be more comfortable than Kitty's little compact. I can make snacks, we can pack a cooler. I'll be your groupie!" I groaned. Just what I needed.

Dad, as usual, focused his attention on Michael. Seemed like lately they were spending a lot of time holed up in Dad's office with the door closed. Something was going on. The air was tense between them. Not relaxed and cozy like the two peas usually were. Once I overheard Dad say, "Stop screwing around, Michael. You have to decide! This isn't the kind of behavior I expect from *you*." A couple of nights later, I heard Michael yell, "I'm not *you*, Dad," and come storming out. I'd never heard Michael yell at Dad. What the heck was going on?

So it was a relief for everyone when Pops showed up.

I was just finishing up with a six-mile run with Max. I dug in for that last bit of energy as we streaked down the street. I lengthened my stride and pumped my arms. I was so focused on my breathing, I didn't notice the white van pulling up alongside me. All of a sudden, I heard a familiar gravelly voice say, "You're doing a sub-seven mile. Pretty damned good for a girl." And there was Pops, grinning, a cigarette hanging out the corner of his mouth, and his cat Ratchet curled on the dashboard.

You know how there's that change that happens between winter and spring? All of a sudden the air smells different, and the light lasts longer. The ice cracks and breaks. Well, that's what it was like whenever Pops showed up. Which is funny if you know Pops.

He's gruff, kind of grouchy. He's not the kind of

grandpa to jiggle you on his knee or wrap you in bear hugs. But he's got his soft spots if you look hard enough and really listen. That night as we all laughed, listening to his stories of life on the road with "an incontinent cat and a canary that was an opera singer in his last life," we didn't notice the late-winter wind racing across the roof and the snow that would eventually pile up five inches. Despite the weather outside, it was spring inside our house.

Whenever Pops stays with us, he always needs things to do. Amy saved up all the little (and not so little) things that need fixing for whenever he came to visit. Leaky faucets; creaky, warped doors; stuck drawers. Amy says that Dad's good at a lot of things, but she gets real nervous when he picks up a hammer or has wiring diagrams in his hands. Not Pops. He can fix anything. "Makes me real popular with the widow women," he says. "And keeps me rolling in casseroles."

Our basement has been in an ongoing state of being finished for years. First Dad wanted to turn it into an office with a bathroom. But that required too much electrical work for Amy's comfort. He managed to put in carpet, hang some Sheetrock here and there, and start what was supposed to be a bathroom. But then that required plumbing. Amy was comical in her relief when Dad announced that if he were going to get tenure, he'd have to stop work on the basement and devote all his time to writing his book instead.

After Michael and I helped carry the last load of Pop's

stuff from the van down to the basement, we watched as he surveyed the half-done mess. He scooped up Ratchet, absently scratching the elderly cat's scarred head. "We got our work cut out for us, boy."

Michael set down the last box. "Sorry, Pops, but between work, school, and lacrosse, I'm not going to be much help." Pops grunted, then looked me up and down. "You'll do," he said.

"Hand me that number-two screwdriver there, Mardie," Pops said, reaching a tattooed arm out from under the sink. Pops had decided that, no matter what else we decided to do with the basement, we'd need a bathroom. I slapped the screwdriver in his palm like I'd seen surgical nurses do on TV.

I sorted through the toolbox, grouping the different screwdrivers, wrenches, pliers, and other stuff in a logical order. "I guess you and Dad did this kind of stuff together all the time when he was a kid."

Pops laughed. "Never," he said. "That boy had no more interest in home repair than you have playing with dolls."

"But I thought you were two peas in a pod, like Dad and Michael."

"Nope," he said, banging on something under the sink. "Your dad always had his nose stuck in a book. He was a lot closer to his mother as a kid. They were a lot alike. Responsible, intellectual homebodies."

"Yeah but, he talks to you all the time and nothing gets him more excited than when you come to visit."

Pops groaned as he slid out from under the sink. He sat up and rubbed the back of his neck. Just like Dad.

He lit a cigarette and studied the ceiling as he blew smoke from his nostrils. "It took a lot of years for your dad and me to be the friends we are now. We both had to do some growing up, to learn to respect how different we are from each other. And how alike."

I sighed. "I don't think Dad and I will ever be friends. Most of the time I don't think he even likes me very much."

One of the things I like about Pops is he doesn't try to talk you out of your feelings. He nodded and said, "People in families don't always like each other, certainly not all the time. I don't doubt that you two butt heads. He's probably not as fair with you as he should be. But there's no doubt in my mind that he loves you."

Pops took me to training Tuesday night. Amy had to cover for someone at the library, and Dad, as usual, was too busy to take me. It would be cool for Pops to see me box, but I'd kind of hoped Dad would go, too.

Kitty and Pops hit it off like they were long lost buds. "You ever watch girl fighters in the ring before?" Kitty asked him.

"Nope," Pops said.

"Well then, you're in for a treat." She turned to me. "Mount up, missy. You're sparring with Destiny tonight."

"Destiny?" I squeaked. I hadn't sparred with her in ages.

"Yep. Shireen's out sick. Cold or something. Besides," she said, putting her arm around my shoulders, "you need a tougher challenge than Shireen. You're ready for the next level."

And sparring with Destiny was definitely the next level. Whereas Shireen was all wild power and emotion, Destiny was exact and calculating. I felt like I was under a microscope. She studied every little thing I did, analyzing all my weaknesses.

At the end of the first round, Kitty said, "She's one cool customer, real different from Shireen."

"No kidding."

"Every boxer you encounter's going to be different. You have to adapt, figure their style and their weakness."

I shook my head. "Her form is perfect. She never drops a hand, never swings wild, and never leaves herself open."

Pops called time from the other corner. Destiny stood up and stretched.

I stood up. Kitty pulled me down to the stool by my wrist. "Remember, Mardie, a person's greatest strength is also their greatest weakness."

A month ago I would have blown her off. But this time I listened and took what she said back into the ring.

Midway through the second round, I figured it out: Destiny analyzed *too much*. She was in her head so much that there were little faults in her timing, and even her foot-work. Then everything clicked into place for me. By the end of the third and last round, she knew she'd been in the ring with Mardie.

Sixteen

The next nine days were a blur of school, running, weights, and training. There wasn't much time for anything else, except my Saturdays at New Horizons.

As I brushed and saddled Feather, Chris, the stable manager, said, "You're on your own today, Mardie. Pete had to go out of town unexpectedly. He said you'd be fine with Feather and Hannah."

"I've never worked with her on my own before."

Chris smiled and waved at Hannah wheeling up the stables corridor, her father behind her. "Pete trusts you."

Hannah's father helped lift her from the wheelchair to Feather's broad back. I positioned the reins in Hannah's one good hand, then placed her feet in the stirrups. "You ready to ride, girlfriend?"

We went slowly around the ring once, my hand supporting her back. I figured that would be all she could handle today. But when I stopped, she flapped her hand and shook her head. It was clear she had other ideas. "You sure you want to ride some more, Hannah?" There was no mistaking what she wanted to do. I looked over at her father. He shrugged. "Let's see if she can go a little longer," he said.

Halfway through her second round, sweat beaded on Hannah's upper lip and forehead, but the look in her eyes was pure determination. I squeezed her waist. "You're doing great." Her body trembled from the effort. "Just a little bit farther . . . ," I said, holding tighter to her hip.

As if sensing her determination, Feather picked up the pace. The three of us had one goal as we moved closer to Hannah's father. By the time we got to his place on the rail, Hannah was quivering, her back drenched in sweat. She slid from Feather's back into her father's arms. He hugged her close, saying, "I'm so proud of you."

I stroked her damp hair. "You're my hero, Hannah.

"Supper's ready, Mardie," Amy called through my bedroom door—for the second time. "Hang up so we can eat."

"I better go," I said to Shireen. "Hope your cold is better soon."

"Yeah, me, too," she said. "I got to get back to the ring to kick your ass."

I laughed. "I miss seeing you, too."

I slid into the chair next to Pops.

"Glad you could join us, Mardie," Dad said.

Pops poked me with an elbow, then winked at Dad. "Better get used to it, Dave. She's at that age. You'll be beating the guys off with a stick." My face turned hot.

"I was talking to *Shireen*, Pops."

He laughed and passed the bowl of mashed potatoes. "And what about you, Michael? Good-lookin' guy like you, I bet you're beating the girls off with a stick."

Everyone looked at their plates.

"Too busy for much of a social life, Pops," Michael said.

Amy rushed in. "That's so true! Between work and school and lacrosse and—"

"Give me a break," Pops said. "No guy his age is 'too busy' for girls." He pointed his forkful of chicken at Michael. "You need to make time for girls, Michael. You don't want people to think you're a fairy or something." Pops laughed, but you could have heard a pin drop. I looked from Amy to Dad, my stomach tight.

Amy stood, grabbing a plate. "Who wants more fried chicken?"

Michael cleared his throat. "Actually, Pops, I *am* gay."

Pops laughed again. "Right." He looked up at Amy, who was clutching the plate to her stomach. Then he looked across the table at Dad, the grin fading from his face.

"He's kidding. Right, Dave?"

Dad shrugged and didn't look at him.

Pops sat back in his chair. He shook his head. "Come on, he can't be gay or whatever they call it now."

"Why not?" I asked. I was actually curious. Why *couldn't* Michael be gay?

"Well for starters, he's a great athlete. I mean, lacrosse isn't a girly-girl game. It's rough."

"So?" I responded.

"And he doesn't talk like one of them. He talks, you know, like a regular guy. And he doesn't act prissy." Here Pops did that limp-wrist thing. "He acts like he's a normal guy."

I looked across the table at Michael. His face went from white to red. His jaw clenched and unclenched. He threw his napkin on the table and started to stand.

"My son *is* normal."

We all looked at Dad. He had been so quiet through all of this, we'd forgotten about him.

"Oh come on, son, you can't believe that. Men with men just isn't right."

Dad looked Pops straight in the eye. "There's nothing wrong with Michael being gay. He's still Michael. He's still my son."

I held my breath.

"But you can't possibly *want* your son to be gay, can you?" Pops asked.

"I want what every parent wants for their children: I want him to be happy, healthy, and able to take care of himself."

Pops blinked, then looked up at Amy. She nodded.

Since it seemed the family was circling the wagons, I threw in my two cents, too. "Besides, Pops, there's lots of weird straight people. Whoever said heteros cornered the market on 'normal'?"

Pops looked around the table. Then he shrugged. "What the hell," he said. "If it doesn't bother you, then I guess it shouldn't bother me."

He looked at Michael. "That doesn't mean I'm thrilled about it. I'm an old guy. You gotta give me some time to wrap my head around this." He stuck his hand across the table to Michael. "Deal?"

Michael shook his hand, hard. "Deal."

It was the Tuesday night before our first match on Saturday. Kitty worked us extra hard. She was kind of driving us nuts.

She watched every little aspect of our footwork, our combinations, our strategy in the ring. "Remember," Kitty said. "In amateur boxing, you win by points, not by knockouts. And you win those points by having the best form, the best technique. By boxing smart."

I'd sure learned a lot about strategy and technique fighting Destiny last week.

Later, as we unwound the wrappings from our hands, Kitty said, "We'll have our last training on Thursday night. I want you to relax Friday night *at home*. Get some rest. Eat a good meal. I'd like to say, 'Don't think about the match,' but I know you will. Just try not to stress about it."

"Yeah, right," Shireen said.

"Look," Kitty said. "This is your first match. Nothing is riding on this. Win or lose, you still go to Denver. The most important thing about this match is getting it over with. You're both virgins."

Shireen laughed. "Excuse me? How you be knowin' 'bout my sex life?"

Kitty rolled her eyes. "You're both virgins when it comes to boxing in competition. You don't know what to expect. You're excited to do it, but scared and nervous, too, right?" We both nodded.

Kitty winked at Pops, who carefully wound up the miles and miles of hand wrap. "You just need to get this first time competing over with. Just think of it as a chance to learn, not something you have to win." Standing, she said, "We'll meet here out front on Saturday morning, seven sharp."

In the locker room, Shireen sat slumped on the bench in her underwear. Usually, she sang and primped in front of the mirror, chattering a mile a minute.

I popped her lightly with my towel. "What's with the *la chica loca*?"

She sighed. "My mom's going to be gone this weekend. Grandma is staying with us Friday and Saturday night."

"So what's the problem?"

She looked at me like I was totally clueless. "Grandma doesn't know how to drive, remember? How am I going to get all the way across town by seven on Saturday morning?"

"Bus?" I ventured.

She shook her head. "Buses don't run that early on Saturday."

I had an idea. "So then you stay with me Friday night."

She sat up. "Stay with you? At your house?"

I laughed. "No. In our garage. Of course in our house, where did you think?"

Shyly, she said, "You should ask your parents first."

I thought about how excited Amy was about the trip to Colorado Springs. It was all she could talk about. "Trust me, it won't be a problem."

Her face broke into a loopy grin.

"But bring your own damn toothbrush," I said. "I don't share."

Alexis called that night. I couldn't remember the last time she'd called me, but I could tell you how many times she hadn't returned *my* calls over the last few months.

"So what's up?" I asked. I squeezed the phone between my ear and shoulder while I untied my shoes.

"Nothing really," she said. "Can't I just call to say hi?"

"Well, it's not exactly something you've done lately," I reminded her.

Ignoring my sarcasm, she said, "So, what are you up to tomorrow night? You want to do something? Maybe a movie or the mall?"

"What's the matter? I thought you and Sam were joined at the hip."

There was a long silence. I was beginning to think she'd hung up on me. Then she said, "Maybe I just felt like hanging out with you instead."

"Well I can't," I said. "I have my first boxing match on Saturday in Colorado Springs. Have to get to bed early and get up early."

"I can't believe you're still doing that, Mardie."

"Doing what?"

"*Boxing*," she said. "People think it's weird."

I laughed. "The people I box with don't think it's weird."

Alexis said in a low voice, "But Mardie, people are saying you're a dyke."

My heart went cold. "That's so stupid. And I hope you've told those assholes that."

Long silence.

"You *did* tell them, didn't you?"

"It's just weird, Mardie. Brittany and Kaylyn said—"

"Who the hell are Brittany and Kaylyn?"

"They're in the drama club. I sit with them at lunch sometimes."

"I don't care what they think," I said.

"I do," Alexis said. "It's . . . well, it's embarrassing, Mardie."

"God forbid I should embarrass you, Alexis." Tears stung my eyes. "I'll try and stay out of you and your little drama queens' orbit." I snapped the cell phone shut. How could she do that to me *again*?

It's funny how things you see every day of your life suddenly look different when you see them through someone else's eyes. Having Shireen stay over at my house Friday night was like flipping through the channels on TV and landing on some lame family sitcom.

There was Dad, the befuddled professor making embarrassing jokes; and Amy, the slightly liberated, witty stepmother clucking around Shireen like a mother hen. Pops sat on the sidelines making wisecracks and saying, "I remember when I was your age." And then, of course, there was my charming gay brother and two predictably adorable dogs. It was disgusting how normal it all was.

Shireen wandered around my room, looking at the books and photographs on my bookshelves. She fingered the curtains and ran her hand over the antique wooden rocking chair that had been my grandmother's. She picked up the photo of my mother.

"Who's this?" she said.

I sprawled back on my bed. "That's my mom."

She studied the photo, then looked at me. "Hmm. You don't look much like her. At least not yet. Your brother looks like her though." Placing the frame carefully back on the dresser she said, "So where is she?"

I gazed up at the ceiling. "Dead."

Shireen curled up in the nest of pillows, sleeping bags, and blankets Amy had brought in.

"How'd she die?" she asked.

"Car accident when I was four. I don't remember her that well."

Shireen sighed. "That's hard. I wouldn't tell anyone else this, but sometimes at night I imagine what it would be like if my father died. The car pulling up in the driveway. The army men in uniforms coming up to the house. You know, like in the movies."

I didn't know what to say.

"I worry about him all the time. It's like, if I can rehearse it all in my head, I won't fall apart when it really happens. I guess that sounds weird. . . ." Shireen fell silent.

A huge fist squeezed down on my heart.

I dragged my pillows and blankets down on the floor next to her. "Let me show you something cool," I said turning off the lights.

"Oh wow, *chica*," Shireen breathed in wonderment as the universe appeared glowing above us in my own little room.

SEVENTEEN

Saturday morning, Amy and Pops loaded the van with a cooler, blankets, pillows, bags of food, several changes of clothes, and our gym bags. For the millionth time, Amy said, "Check your bags, girls. Make sure you have your gloves, mouthpieces, water bottles, shoes—"

"Amy, just chill," I said. "You had us check our bags two minutes ago, and two minutes before *that*. Nothing's changed!"

Finally, it was time to go. "Get on out here, girls. Kitty's waiting on us," Pops shouted.

As I started out the door, Dad called, "Mardie, wait a minute."

Dad. It's a funny thing. I knew in my heart of hearts he wouldn't come to the match. I told myself I didn't care. Why should I? But that morning, a little movie played over and over in my head: Dad coming down to the kitchen and saying, "What are we all sitting around here for? We've got a match to go to!" But, of course, it was just a stupid fantasy.

Dad looked down at his shoes and said, "I'm sorry I won't be there for your first match, bug. Michael's got a game today. I can't be in two places at once. . . ." His voice trailed off.

I shrugged, not looking at him. "Sure, Dad."

I could feel his eyes on me. "I'll come to the next one." *Right*.

I stepped off the front porch, the sky still studded with stars.

"Be safe, Mardie," Dad called. "Keep your hands up."

I fumed the whole drive over, as Destiny and Shireen slept, Kitty and Amy talked softly in the front, and Pops snored next to me. Michael's game was in Lewiston, only a half hour away. Michael could drive himself, for god's sake. He'd been to every freaking game of Michael's for the past four years, but he couldn't come to my first match. Real supportive, Dad. Just great.

Then this creepy, cold little voice in my head said, *Why would he want to waste his time on a loser?*

The match was held at the local high school. In the middle of the gym, flanked by tables for the judges and the fight physician, sat a temporary boxing ring.

Kitty introduced us to the Colorado Springs coach, a tall redhead named Louisa. She smiled and said, "We're glad you girls could make it. My girls have been chomping at the bit to get some matches in before Denver. Glad you could oblige."

What ranch did she come off of?

Kitty smiled. "Be careful what you wish for. These girls ain't nobody's warm-up partners. They're here to win."

"What happened to 'you're just here to learn?'" Shireen whispered.

I felt queasy. My mouth full of cotton balls.

It was a lot of hurry up and wait. The first clipboard official checked our USA Boxing passbooks, scribbled something on the inside, and scurried away. The next clipboard checked our passbooks, our parental permission slips, and wrote down our date of birth. Kitty signed off at the bottom.

Next came the weigh-in and the check with the fight physician. The doc shined a little light in my eyes, ears, down my throat. Checked me over for any cuts or sores. He scribbled something on his clipboard and smiled. "You're good to go, Miss Wolfe," he said. "Be safe out there." Maybe now we'd get this show on the road.

But no. We were herded to the equipment room. Chest protectors, headgear, and gloves were piled high on the tables. I couldn't believe the amount of time the girls from this club were taking to find just the right chest protector. I wanted to scream, "It's a boxing match, not a friggin' fashion show!" By the time we got back to the locker room, my stomach was in knots.

As I finally started wrapping my hands, Kitty sauntered over with *her* clipboard. "No need to start wrapping up yet, Mardie. The guys box first."

"What?"

"Yep. There'll be four guys competing before you gals go out."

"But I thought this was only girls. Why are guys fighting?" I sounded like a whiny little kid.

Kitty looked at me, one eyebrow raised. "No, I told you the other night this was a mixed club. They only have three girls. Not much sense setting up all this for just three matches. Besides," she said, rolling up the tan hand-wrap, "you can learn something from watching the guys. It'll give you a feel for what it's like out there, with people watching and all." *Christ*. I put my head in my hands.

Kitty put her arm around my shoulders and gave me a little shake. "Come on, Mardie. Relax. You're psyching yourself out. Look at Destiny and Shireen."

I looked up. Destiny was over in the corner with one of her Sudoku books. Shireen was chatting it up with another Latino girl like they were at a party or something.

"You need to relax, Mardie. You've been wound up ever since we got here."

I shrugged off her arm. "I want to win." She considered me for a moment. "Want or *need*, Mardie?"

She called Destiny and Shireen over. "Okay, you fight in order of weight class, so Destiny goes first, Shireen second, Mardie last."

Great. More time to wait.

"Destiny, you've boxed Lisa before at last year's state finals, so you know what you're up against." Destiny nodded as she braided her hair back.

"Shireen, the girl you're matched up with is a newbie, too. She hasn't boxed in a match before, but she's an ex–kick-boxing competitor, so watch out." Shireen snapped her gum and grinned.

Then she looked at me. "Mardie, the girl you'll be in the ring with has already won two matches. I've seen her and she's good. But she's not as quick or as smart as you. And she doesn't have your reach."

Looking each of us in the eye, she said, "I brought the three of you here because you're the best. You have heart, tons of talent, and you're braver than any of those folks in the stands will ever be. Whatever happens out there in the ring today, you'll all be winners. And you'll learn more than you might think." She stood and clapped her hands. "Now, let's all go out there and show them Kitty's girls are here."

It was a good thing Destiny went first, because she taught the idiots in the stands a thing or two. One minute into the first round, she shut them up with her strong, methodical work. When she caught the other girl with a quick uppercut that sent her to her knees, murmurs of admiration rippled through the stands. Destiny won her match by a mile.

Shireen was not the same person in this ring I had sparred with countless times. Gone were the wild swings, unpredictable combinations, and flashing, angry eyes. In other words, *la chica loca* was not in the ring. This Shireen was actually relaxed, focused, and enjoying herself. Unfortunately, the ex–kick boxer was not quite as relaxed as Shireen, and in even better shape. Shireen lost her match by a small margin. But she still came out grinning ear to ear.

And then it was my turn. All that time waiting, and now The Moment rushed toward me like an oncoming train.

"Okay, Mardie," Kitty said, rubbing my shoulders.

"The ref is going to give you the rules. You'll touch gloves, come back to your corner. When the bell rings—"

"Fighters to center ring, please."

Kitty gave me a little shove.

I barely heard the ref's instructions over the hammering of my heart. The girl and I touched gloves. The ref had to remind me to go back to my corner. Laughter rose from the stands.

I stumbled back to my corner. Kitty talked in my ear, but I don't remember a thing she said. What I do remember is looking up in the stands and seeing who wasn't there.

The bell rang.

"Go, Mardie," Kitty said.

I thought I was going to puke.

The girl danced out to the middle of the ring on the balls of her feet. She looked light as a feather. I, on the other hand, felt like I was wading through wet concrete.

Her arm shot out, popped me on the shoulder, and then she danced away. She struck me again, and again danced away.

I knew just what she was doing. She was testing me to see where my weak spots were, what my reach was like. I'd done it a million times, sparring.

But in my first real competition ever, all I could do was keep my gloves pinned in front of my face. It was like they were locked tight in place.

"Come on and fight," someone yelled from the stands.

Shireen yelled from the sidelines, "You go, girl! Show her what you got!" and even Destiny called out, "You can do it, Mardie."

The girl moved in, pressed me to the ropes. I swung wildly with my left, barely touching her helmet.

She slammed her fist just below my ribs. "Fight, damn it," she hissed around her mouthpiece.

I tucked my chin and managed to nail her with an uppercut just as the bell rang.

I collapsed in my corner, as much out of shame as exhaustion. I wondered if anyone would notice if I slunk out of there and went home.

Kitty squirted water in my mouth and over my shoulders. "Come on, Mardie," she said. "You're getting the best of yourself! You're good enough to beat this girl!"

But Dad didn't think I was good enough to come and watch. I felt like I was right back in the gym, that night when Ben and Sam saw me in the ring. Huge, stupid-looking gloves hung at the end of long skinny arms. I looked like a freak.

The bell rang again. "Go show them who you are," Kitty said.

But I knew I was a clown, a loser.

So I lost. And not by a small margin. The only good thing I can say for myself and that match was I went the full three rounds, and I did leave a pretty good goose egg on that smug girl's pretty face.

And then it was over.

Pops treated everyone to pizza before we started the drive home.

"Let's debrief, ladies," Kitty said. "Destiny, what did you learn out there this afternoon?"

I sighed. What was the point of asking Destiny? Her match was flawless.

"Even though I'd fought her before, it was still like fighting a new person. She had improved a lot since last year. I underestimated her at first," Destiny said.

Kitty nodded. "Shireen?"

Shireen was still grinning like an idiot, even though she'd lost. She wolfed down her third huge slice.

"You looked like a different person out there today," Kitty said. "What was different?"

Shireen wiped tomato sauce off her shirt. "Yeah, that was weird, wasn't it? But it was like, I wasn't *angry* out there. I was just enjoying it."

Destiny said, "*La chica loca* wasn't there."

"Yeah," Shireen said, staring off into a middle space. Then she said, "I don't know . . . I just felt good up there today. I was okay." Destiny nodded.

Then they all looked at me. I looked down at the wet rings on the table. I shrugged and said, "Guess I learned I'm not cut out for competition."

Kitty snorted. "Now you listen to me, missy. It takes a loss in the ring for any boxer to become stronger mentally, physically, and emotionally. Losing just makes you want to win more. Either that, or it makes you want to quit. And I don't see any quitters sitting at this table."

Shireen flung an arm around my shoulders, still clutching a pizza slice. "Oh come on, *blanca*. I lost, too. So what? You'll win the next one. You'll kick ass in Denver."

I pushed her arm off and got up to go to the bathroom. "I'm not going to Denver." As they all stared at me in disbelief, in disappointment, I could hear Dad's voice saying, "Mardie never sticks with anything."

We loaded up in the van for the long drive home. To my surprise and relief, Destiny crawled into the back with me. *Good*, I thought. *At least I'll have peace and quiet.*

I dreaded going home. There Dad would be, all excited about Michael's lacrosse win, and me having to admit I lost. I just wanted a little quiet time to be miserable.

"Who were you fighting out there today?" I jumped at the sound of Destiny's voice. I thought she was asleep.

"What do you mean?" I asked, even though I knew trying to game Destiny was useless.

Another long silence. Then she said, "I'm guessing your dad."

I stared out the cold window and up at the indifferent stars. Headlights of cars flickered by.

"I know what it's like to feel you need to win to prove to someone that you're worth loving."

I just shrugged. I didn't need this.

"My father was never even in my life. He left the day after I was born. We never saw his sorry ass again."

I looked at her in the faint light of the car. Glancing at

me she said, "My mom did the best she could. So did my grandparents. But I still ended up a mess. Kitty and boxing saved me."

She bowed her head, picked her short fingernails. "Still, when I first started competing, I was fighting for my father, so I lost all the time."

"Why would you fight for a father you never knew?" I asked

She sighed. "Just because he was a selfish bastard didn't change the fact I needed him to love me."

We both thought this over. Then I said, "But you *do* win."

She nodded. "Took me a long time to figure out some things, though, before I started winning."

"Like what?" I asked.

"I had to figure out *why* I was boxing and what I really needed from it. Once I figured that out, I started winning."

I remembered Kitty asking me if I *needed* to win or *wanted* to win.

As if reading my mind, Destiny said, "You can't *need* to win, Mardie. It's too much to carry into the ring. *Wanting* to win is a whole 'nother matter."

"Do you want to win now?" I asked.

She smiled for the first time that night. "In the worst way."

"Why?" I whispered. "Why do you want to win?"

"Because *I'm* good enough," she said. "I don't need to prove anything to anybody else. I just want to be the best I can be."

"Hey, everybody, we're home," Amy called out. The house was quiet. No Dad bouncing around the kitchen talking nonstop about what a great game Michael had. No stereo blaring opera from Michael's room. No happy greetings from the dogs.

Amy and Pops looked at each other, puzzled.

A door opened down the hall. Dad came out of his office. He gave Amy a tired kiss on the cheek. "How'd it go, bug?" he asked.

Without looking at him, I said, "I lost my match."

"I'm sorry, Mardie," he said. "I know how hard you trained. There're other matches coming up, though, right?"

Before I had a chance to tell him I was quitting boxing, Amy said, "How'd the lacrosse game go? How badly did Michael's team beat Lewiston?"

Here we go. No way did I want to stand around and hear about how great Michael was. I grabbed my gym bag to head to my room.

"They didn't. Michael got thrown out of the game."

I stopped midstep and dropped my bag.

I couldn't believe what Dad had just said. Neither could Amy. "You're kidding," she said.

Dad sat down wearily at the breakfast bar. He shook his head. "Halfway through the second half, he jumped a guy. He's suspended for the next two games."

"I'll be damned," Pops said. "Who would've thought."

"But guys are always getting in fights during the games, Dave," Amy said. "They don't get suspended. That hardly seems fair—"

"It wasn't one of the other players, Amy," Dad said, cutting her off. "It was a guy on the sidelines. A spectator. Apparently he'd said things to Michael during halftime. Something he said set Michael off."

"Those Lewiston fans can be nasty," Amy said uncertainly.

Dad picked up a ceramic cup I made when I was six. He ran his thumb across its lumpy side. "That's the thing. It wasn't some jerk from Lewiston. It was someone from here."

The hair stood up on the back of my neck. "Who was it?" I asked.

"Eric Lindstrom."

"Holy crap," I breathed. They all looked at me.

"Is Michael in his room?" I asked.

Dad nodded.

I padded down to Michael's room and tapped on the door. "Michael, can I come in?" Silence. Teddy whined, sniffed under the door. "Come on, Michael," I said. "It's just me. I promise." I heard a grumble. He opened the door a crack, motioning me in.

I hadn't been in Michael's room in years. We used to hang out in each other's rooms all the time. But once puberty hit (did gay guys have puberty?), we never set foot in each other's rooms again.

The thing that surprised me the most was how much his room looked like mine. Posters on the wall (foreign films rather than rock bands), bookshelves stuffed with books and trophies (lacrosse rather than soccer). He even had a framed photograph of our mom on his dresser.

Shoving his hands in his pockets, he said, "No doubt you've heard about my fall from grace."

I perched on the edge of his bed. "Sounds like it was Eric who took the fall. What was that asshole doing there, anyway?"

"Who knows," Michael said, sitting down on the floor with the dogs. Teddy curled up in his lap, sniffing his chin. "I heard he has a cousin or something who plays for Lewiston. I've seen him at games before. He's always talking trash."

"Must have been a bucket-load for you to jump on him. I must be a bad influence on you."

Michael buried his nose in Teddy's thick fur. "Let's just say I'd had enough."

"Did you break his nose?" I asked, half joking, half not.

"No, they pulled us apart before I could break anything. But his face isn't quite as pretty as it used to be."

"Jesus, Michael," I said. "What did he say to inspire that?"

He lay back on the floor and stared up at his own star-studded ceiling. "Same old stuff those kind of guys always say. 'Fag,' 'queer boy,' 'mother lover.' That wasn't so much what set me off."

"What was it then?" I asked.

At first it seemed like he wasn't going to answer. Then he said, "It was when he started talking about you."

I was so shocked, I almost fell off the bed. Michael defending me? "God, Michael, you didn't have to do that."

He sat up. "Don't flatter yourself too much," he said. "It was just the proverbial last straw. I'm just sick of the whole thing, the whole trash-talking, macho attitude of those guys. Just between you and me, I'm glad to be suspended. I've been thinking about quitting anyway. This is the perfect out."

"Quit?" I said. "You can't quit! Then you give assholes like Eric just want they want!"

"I'm sick of it, Mardie. I've been playing lacrosse for five years now. The only reason I've stuck with it is Dad."

"Dad?"

"Yeah. I don't want to disappoint him. It's been bad enough for him that I'm gay. If I tell him I don't want to play lacrosse anymore, he'll write me off altogether."

"Hey, all things considered, Dad's taken the whole gay thing pretty well. It's not like he's hauled you off to a shrink or kicked you out of the house."

Michael raised his eyebrows.

"I know, I know. I'm usually the last one to defend Dad, but it's true. I don't think you could ever do *anything* to disappoint him. After all, you're the other half of the two peas," I said.

Michael shook his head. He stood up, wandered around the room. He picked up a photo of him and Dad, arms flung around each other's shoulders, grinning. With his back to me, he said, "That's just it, Mardie. I don't *want* to be one of the two peas anymore. The things I want to do and *not* do are going to kill Dad."

"What, you want to move to San Fran and have a sex change operation?" I asked.

Michael laughed. "Well, not quite that bad."

"Then what?"

Michael turned to me. He still clutched the framed photo to his chest. "I want to be a veterinarian, I think. Maybe."

"Well, that is different from going into history and academics like Dad has all planned out for you, but it's not like you're blowing off college."

Silence. "Michael?"

More silence. "You aren't, are you?"

He sat next to me on the bed. "That's the worst part," he said. "I *don't* want to go to college. At least not right away. I need to take a break, Mardie. I'm tired. I've spent twelve years being the best, doing what everyone else wanted me to do. But I'm sick of school. I want to take at least a year off. Figure some things out."

What could I say? If Michael had told me he wanted to move to India, shave his head, and weave baskets, I couldn't have been more surprised. So I just kept nodding my head, not knowing what else to do.

"I do have a plan though. Sort of."

"And that would be?"

Taking a deep breath, he said, "You remember Dad's student from Scotland?"

"Sure. Dylan McSomething?"

Michael nodded. "We're going to Europe right after graduation to travel for a few months. He's going to show me all these cool places in Scotland, too. I've saved up tons of money. Then, when I get back, I'm moving to Georgia."

"Georgia?"

Picking up steam, he said, "Yeah! Jan says I can work with her at her vet clinic. She needs the extra hands, and it would help me figure out if being a vet is really what I want to do. She says she'll pay me a little bit, plus room and board."

So that's what they were talking about at Christmas.

"Then," he continued, "if I decide I want to be a vet, she said she can get me some good contacts at Auburn University. That's where she went."

"Wow," I said. "Sounds like you've got this all figured out."

He slumped down next to me, resting his head on my shoulder. "Yeah, except I can't bring myself to tell Dad. So instead I keep putting off applying to schools and now he's pissed."

"So just tell him," I said.

"Easy for you to say," he sighed. "You're a lot braver than me."

I gave him a shove. "Get outta here. I'm not *brave*. You've heard Dad. I'm a fuckup."

Michael sat up and looked me straight in the eye. "No, Mardie, you're brave. If I'd been you, I wouldn't have waited so many years to tell Dad I was gay. If I were you, I wouldn't care what Dad thought about my going to college or not."

I wanted to say, "But I *do care*, maybe too much, what Dad thinks." But I didn't. Instead I wagged my finger at him. "Argue for your limitations and they're yours."

Michael blinked. "What? Argue for your limitations and what?"

I repeated it.

He shook his head and threw his arm around me. "When did you get so smart?"

We stayed up late into the night, talking. By the time I crawled out of bed the next morning, most everyone was gone. Michael had gone to work. Amy left a note saying she and Dad were running errands. As I poured honey into my tea, Pops came up from the basement.

"'Bout time you got out of bed. Everybody else has flown the coop. I need your help down in the basement."

I groaned. "I'm too sore from yesterday, Pops."

"Easy work today. We're slapping on that wallpaper Amy picked out. Besides, I'm leaving tomorrow. Gotta get this done."

My heart sank at the thought of Pops leaving.

We worked easily together. Once we got a rhythm going, wallpapering was kind of fun. My mind wandered. Then I found myself asking him out of the blue, "Pops, what was my mother like?"

Pops brushed sticky goo in one corner. "To be honest, I didn't know your mom all that well. Seemed like I was always busy when she and your dad came out to visit. She was a beautiful woman, though. Had a great laugh. You sound like her when you laugh."

He climbed down from the ladder, taking the wallpaper I'd measured and cut. He studied me closely for a minute, head cocked. "Can't see much of her in you, except maybe a little around the mouth and eyes. And you got her height." He climbed back up the ladder, then said over his shoulder, "You were a little thing when she died. You must not remember much."

"No," I said, measuring and cutting.

"Your dad's told you about her, hasn't he?"

I handed the sheet of wallpaper up to him. "Only time he ever even mentions her," I said, "is when I screw up. Then he says, 'Jesus Christ, Mardie! You're just like your mother!'"

Pops chuckled. "Pretty good imitation of your old man."

He climbed back down and stretched his back. "Let's go outside and take a break from this glue. I need a smoke."

We sat side by side on the top steps of the deck. The sun was bright. There was a warmth in the air I hadn't felt in a long time. It finally felt like spring. Real spring.

Pops took a deep drag on his cigarette, slowly exhaling. "I think the reason your dad doesn't talk about her is because he feels guilty."

"Guilty about what?" I asked.

He stubbed out his cigarette. "Your mom was a nice person," he said. "Life-of-the-party type. But she had her problems. Like I said, I didn't know her that well, but your dad talked with your grandma and then she'd tell me."

Picking at a piece of loose paint, I said, "Yeah, Michael said they fought a lot."

Pops nodded. "Yep. I think your mother was one of those people always looking for something to make her happy. She tried lots of different things—selling cosmetics, opening a little restaurant. She even went back to college for a little while, but she didn't stick with it. All those things cost your dad money."

I flicked the piece of paint away angrily. "Dad's a real tightwad. Even Amy says so."

"Your dad had reason to be, then. He had student loans to pay off, had just started teaching and had two small children. Anyway," he continued, "she started drinking, going off at night and leaving you kids with him. It got pretty bad. They got into a big fight one night. He told her if she didn't start acting more like a mother, he'd divorce her. She took off, went drinking with her friends. Coming home, she drove her car off a bridge. Killed instantly. I think your dad's always felt if he hadn't had that fight with her, she might not have gone out that night."

We were quiet for a long moment. Then he said, "The point is, most everyone in the world is doing the best they can with what they have. That was true of your mother and it's true of your father. But that's no excuse for him not to tell you about her. She had her good points. Everyone does. And everyone needs to know where they come from."

Tears swam across my eyes. "I never even knew her and I miss her. It's stupid."

Pops put his arm around me and pulled me to him. "It's not stupid. You need to know who she was."

Holding me away from him, he said, "What *would* be stupid would be for you to quit boxing. Your dad's never been a quitter and neither are you. You're *part* your mother, part your father. But you are one hundred percent Mardie Wolfe, warts and all. Don't you ever forget that."

EIGHTEEN

Still, I couldn't make myself go to training that next week. I was in a world-class funk.

Spring was happening all around me, and all I could do was drag my sorry butt to school and back home again. Couldn't find the energy to return Shireen's and Rick's phone calls. Even Alexis called again, but I just didn't care.

Thursday night, Dad and I picked at our salads as Amy hummed in the kitchen. Dad was in a funk this week, too. Ever since Pops left, he'd hardly been out of his office. A couple of times when I walked past his open door, I saw him just sitting at his desk, staring into space.

When Michael finally got off the phone, Amy served up steaming plates of spaghetti. A couple of bites later, Michael cleared his throat. "I need to have a family meeting," he said, looking at Dad.

Dad put down his fork and wiped his mouth. "Sure. Can it wait, though? I have some work I need to finish up."

Glancing at me, Michael said, "Now, Dad. I need to

talk *now*. And I need you to just listen. Hear me out before you try to talk me out of what I want to do."

The color drained from Dad's face.

Michael took a deep breath, glanced at me again, then said in one big rush, "I'm not going to college this year, Dad, and I don't want to be a history professor like you. I want different things for myself than you want for me."

Wow.

Dad's face reddened.

Amy leaned forward. "Okay, so you've told us what all you're *not* going to do. What *are* you going to do?"

As Michael laid out his plans for a summer in Europe and next year in Georgia, I watched disappointment, doubt, anger, resignation, and then a hint of curiosity march across my father's face. Me, I was proud of my brother: a pea no longer.

A last blast of winter blew in Saturday morning, lashing the windows with a mixture of ice, snow, and rain. "That's life in the high country," Amy said, as she bundled up for a walk.

I almost didn't go to New Horizons that day. Both Rick and Lizzie were sick with colds. I just wanted to stay buried underneath my covers. But Amy made it clear that if I stayed home, she'd keep me busy. Given a choice between spending the day cleaning toilets and closets or going to the center . . . well, what do you think I chose?

"Guess this storm's keeping everybody home," Pete said in the tack room. "Surprised you came out. But I'm glad you did. It will be a good day to give the stalls a scrub down."

Great. Might as well have stayed home.

So we were both surprised a little later when we heard Feather's gentle nicker, the one he used to greet Hannah. Pete was knee-deep cleaning one stall, and I was just finishing up another. I wiped my hands on my jeans and stuck my head over the stall door. Wheeling up the breezeway were Hannah and her dad.

"I didn't want to come out in this weather," Hannah's dad said. "Figured it'd be best to stay off the roads, but Hannah wasn't hearing any excuses. She would have walked here herself if I'd let her."

Pete and I laughed. "No problem," Pete said, ruffling Hannah's fine brown hair, something I happen to know she hates. "I think Feather would have been unhappy if you didn't show up today."

Feather sensed something different that day. As Pete and I settled Hannah into the saddle and hooked her boots in the stirrups, Feather, usually so mellow, was almost quivering. Pete glanced at me with raised eyebrows. I shrugged.

I put the reins in Hannah's good hand, patted her leg, and started to make a joke when I looked at her. Her face was set, her eyes fixed on the clock on the far side of the ring. Let me tell you, if you looked up *determination* in your dictionary, you'd see a picture of Hannah. I touched her arm. "What're you planning? Is today the day you ride thirty minutes?"

One lap around the ring, then two, then three. Five minutes, ten. At the fifteen-minute mark, Hannah's dad and Pete stopped their conversation and watched.

I felt her muscles quiver underneath my hand. "You can do it, Hannah," I said. "You're strong enough." She glanced down at me, tightened her good hand on the reins. If I didn't know better, I'd swear she gave Feather a little nudge in the ribs with her boots.

Twenty-two minutes. The longest she'd ever ridden. Feather picked up the pace. I watched Hannah, then realized I was holding my breath. I wrapped my arm a little farther around her waist and rested my hand on her stomach. Synchronized my breathing with hers. "Deep breaths, Hannah. Deep breaths. We can do this."

Twenty-five minutes. Hannah was drenched in sweat, her face red, almost contorted with determination. She squeezed her eyes shut. I willed the hands on the clock to move faster. *Please don't let her fall*, I prayed over and over.

Pete and her father walked into the ring. "Hannah, stop," her father called. "I don't want you to overdo it." I waved him off. "Let her do this."

Hannah opened her eyes, fixing on the clock. One minute to go.

"You're going to do it, Hannah!" I said, squeezing her waist.

One last time, she glanced down at me. With surprising strength, she pushed my arm away. Stunned, I stopped, and watched Hannah ride without anyone's help. Back quivering but erect, hand flapping, grinning ear to ear. For those last few seconds, I walked close, but didn't touch her.

Pete and Hannah's dad lifted her off Feather's back. I watched as these two big, grown men fussed and laughed over this little girl like proud mother hens.

As Pete and I watched Hannah and her dad wheel across the breezeway, Pete said, "I never in a million years thought she could do it. Did you?"

I watched Hannah's dad leaning down close, talking in Hannah's ear. "Doesn't matter what we thought. She never stopped believing she could do it."

As soon as I got home, I laced up my neglected running shoes and headed out. If Hannah wouldn't give up, then why should I? I'd call Rick and see if he wanted to go to a movie.

I trotted down our road and hit my stride. I felt good. I felt like myself again.

NINETEEN

When I showed up at the gym Tuesday night, Shireen whooped with delight, Kitty grinned and nodded. "I knew you'd be back."

"What made you so sure?" I asked as I wrapped my hands.

"I've known you up close and personal for six months now. You're no quitter. You just needed a little break. An attitude adjustment."

"Maybe so," I said.

After a grueling two hours of hitting the bags, weights, and sparring, Kitty said, "Let's talk about your next match before you hit the showers. You two will be fighting at the Pueblo boxing club in two weeks. It's a new club. I don't know the coach there, but she's got a good reputation. I don't think the girls you're matched up with are very experienced."

"Sounds good," Shireen said.

"Can be," Kitty said, nodding. "But you should never underestimate your opponent. So I want you two to train these next two weeks like you mean it."

I felt a small thrill at the idea of training intensely for this. "We're out for spring break that week before we go to Pueblo. I can come every day."

Shireen nodded. "I gotta hang with the sibs some of that time, but I'll be down here whenever I can get away."

"What about Destiny?" I asked. "Isn't she going to fight?"

"No," Kitty said. "Nobody at that club she could be matched with. It'd just be a waste of her time. She's going to work one of your corners." I hoped it would be mine.

"Mardie, you think Amy will be willing to help us out again with transportation?"

I laughed. "We couldn't keep her away, even if we wanted to. She thinks she's our groupie or something."

Later, as Amy drove across town to drop Shireen off at her house, we talked about Pueblo.

Amy said, "You're going to stay over with us the night before, aren't you?"

Shireen said, "That all right with you, Mardie?"

I hooked my finger and popped her bra strap that had slipped, as usual, down one shoulder. "Yeah, I guess." I said. "But don't make a habit out of it."

Friday, everyone at school was hyper and friendlier than usual. The cafeteria was practically a lovefest. The usual grunts and postures from the Jock Table were turned down to low volume. The Geeks and Suffering Artists sat together. Nothing like a warm, spring day to ratchet up the niceness quotient.

Like a cat seeking a sunny spot, I took a sun-bathed table on the fringe. My stomach grumbled as I unwrapped my chicken salad sandwich.

"Hey," a small voice said.

I looked up. Alexis.

I almost made a sarcastic remark about her being hard up for company, until I noticed how freaked she looked. I cleared my stuff to the side. "Hey, yourself," I said. "Want to sit?"

She sat down, barely looking at me. I noticed she didn't have any lunch. "Want half my sandwich? It's Amy's chicken salad."

"No, thanks," she said, picking at one badly chewed nail.

"Oh come on," I said, giving her half anyway. "You always loved her chicken salad sandwiches. And her egg salad sandwiches, and her tuna salad sandwiches. You know what she always says," I said, prompting a long-standing joke among the three of us.

Alexis smiled a little. "Yet another vehicle for mayonnaise."

She looked so small, so defeated sitting there. "So what's up?" I asked.

She looked at me with those big green eyes that usually danced with mischief. Then she said those two dreaded words. "I'm pregnant."

My heart fell from my chest to my stomach. "Holy shit," I said.

"At least, I think I am. I'm late."

"How late?" I asked.

"Three weeks," she said. "And I feel sick to my stomach all the time."

"Crap," I said. "What are you going to do?"

"I need your help, Mardie."

She glanced around the cafeteria, then leaned in and whispered, "I need you to lift one of those home pregnancy tests for me from the drugstore."

I sat back. "By 'lift' I assume you mean—"

"Steal it, Mardie. You know how."

I stood up so fast, my chair fell back. "Forget it," I said.

The cafeteria was suddenly quiet. Everyone stared at us.

I grabbed my backpack. I pushed open the door to the outside commons. I wanted to scream. I wanted to run. I couldn't believe she was asking me to do this.

"Mardie."

I didn't have to turn around. I knew who it was: the one person I would do anything for. Without looking at Alexis, I said, "I'll come over to your house later this afternoon."

"You'll get it?" she asked.

I swallowed down a sour taste burning its way up my throat. "Yeah," I said.

The bell rang for next class. I turned, facing her.

Not looking at me, she said, "You're a good friend, Mardie. I'm sorry I haven't been so nice to you these past few months."

I shrugged on my backpack. "I'll see you this afternoon."

THE RING

I wandered the aisles of the drugstore, picking up shampoos, then putting them down. I examined the labels on hair remover like it was the most fascinating reading on earth. It would be so easy to slip something in my pocket. I wasn't even sure the cashier would sell a home pregnancy test to me. Wasn't there a law or something that you had to be eighteen to buy one of those things?

On the other hand, it felt like every freakin' person in that store was watching me. I wanted to yell, "People change! I'm not a loser!" But I couldn't, even if I wanted to. I felt like I was going to puke.

Taking a deep breath, I headed to the sign that read FEMININE HYGIENE. What a stupid name. There, all grouped together, were pads and tampons, various creams and gels. And way too many different types of home pregnancy tests.

I grabbed a bright pink box that said it was 99 percent accurate. Good enough for me.

I stuffed the box in my pocket, drew myself up tall, and walked over to the pharmacy cash register.

I placed the box on the counter like I bought these things all the time. The lady behind the counter glanced at the box, then looked up at me.

I tried my best to look eighteen. She studied me too long for comfort, then sighed and punched some keys on the register.

"That'll be nineteen fifty," she said.

I counted out the money and shoved it across the counter. "It's for a friend," I said.

She bagged up the pink box. "It always is," she said.

Alexis answered the door before I rang the bell. I held up the bag. "You owe me nineteen bucks." I stepped into the doorway.

She pushed me back. "Not here," she whispered. "My mom's home."

"I'm going over to Mardie's, Mom," she called over her shoulder.

Alexis's mom called from the kitchen, "Be home for dinner, Alexis. Mardie, tell Amy to call me."

Before I could answer, Alexis shoved me out the door.

We huddled together on the edge of the bathtub. We stared hard at the test strip in Alexis's hand.

"Read the instructions again," Alexis said, eyes locked on the little strip.

"It says, 'Pass the test strip through your urine stream—'"

"Not *that* part of the instructions, Mardie! The results part."

"Let's see. Okay, it says, 'If you are pregnant, a plus sign will appear in the middle of the strip. If you are not pregnant—'"

"Oh my god, is it a minus sign? Please tell me it's a minus sign, Mardie."

I looked at the strip in her hand. Sure enough, right there in the middle was a minus sign. A big, beautiful minus sign. "You're not pregnant, Alexis," I whispered.

Alexis whooped so loud the dogs came running. She threw up her arms, pumped her fists. "I'm NOT PREG-NANT!" and slid backward into the tub, laughing.

I slid down next to her. She grabbed my hand, squeezed it hard. She hiccuped, leaned her head against my arm. "Oh, my god," she said. "I feel like my head's been taken off the chopping block. Like the governor called with a last-minute reprieve."

"Yeah, you're lucky," I said. Her legs stuck up straight in the air; mine folded over the side of the bathtub. "But what would you have done if—"

Alexis groaned. "Let's not even go there, Mardie."

"But didn't you think about what you'd do when you thought you might be pregnant?"

"Woulda, shoulda, coulda," Alexis said. "I'm not preg-nant, so what does it matter now?"

"Yeah, but—"

She pulled away. "Let's celebrate my life as we know it *not* being over. What should we do?"

I thought for a second. I stood and pulled her to her feet. "Let's go get a burger and shoot some pool at Smitty's."

TWENTY

Sunday, as I sat on the bottom step lacing up my running shoes, psyching myself up for a long, hard run, Dad came up behind me. "Mind if I join you on your run, bug?" he asked.

I wasn't sure how I could say no, since he already had his running shoes and stuff on.

"I could use a good workout," he said, patting his slightly bulging belly. "Work off some of this hibernation fat."

Right, I thought. *You want a workout? I'll give you a workout.*

We took the long, meandering roads that led out of town through rolling hills dotted with subdivisions.

Dad told me all about how when he first moved to South Eden twenty years ago, it was all sheep and horse ranches; how the old family lands were gradually sold off and turned into pricey, high-end second-home "ranchettes" for people from Denver looking to have a "real" Western experience.

After about four miles, we took the road that swung

back toward the west end of town near the high school. Looming up ahead was Miner's Hill. We could see the two huge, white intersecting M's carved into the side of the hill. The symbol for our school football team, the Mighty Miners.

Dad chattered away about his early days in South Eden. He didn't have a clue where I was taking him.

Miner's Hill may technically be a hill, but it's a killer. It has six switchbacks from bottom to top. For some twisted reason, I love running that hill, but it can be brutal. It was going to kick Dad's butt.

He'd stopped talking. Sweat beaded on his upper lip. When I swung on to the trail he said, "You're kidding, right?"

I shook my head. "I run this all the time. But if you're not up to it, we can turn around."

He got that stubborn look that drives Amy crazy. "If you're up for it, so am I," he said.

I just hoped my plan wouldn't backfire and give him a heart attack or something.

We worked our way up through the switchbacks, past sagebrush and pinion pines. We startled a couple of bunnies. Even a deer.

I set a brutal pace. On purpose. I dug in, but so did he.

By about the fourth switchback, he'd fallen a couple paces behind. I could hear him breathing harder. But he didn't say a word, didn't quit.

We made the top in what was probably my best time. My legs hurt and my lungs burned.

Dad bent over at the waist, panting. Sweat streamed

off the end of his nose, his face red. "Jesus, Mardie," he said panting. "You trying to knock off your old man?"

I laughed and patted his wet back. "What's the matter, Dad? Can't keep up with a girl?"

He stood up straight and smiled at me. "Not just *any* girl. The Wolfe." We laughed together for the first time in a long time.

"Let's take a breather, bug," he said, sitting on a couch-sized boulder.

I sat next to him and felt a wonderfully cool breeze across my bare neck. "Miner's Hill has a great view," I said.

Dad opened his eyes and took in the scene before us. He nodded. "Yep, there's the college. I think I can even see the history building."

"And over there's the library and the New Horizons Center," I said.

We pointed out other landmarks: the elementary and junior high schools, the post office, skating rink, movie theaters, shopping mall.

Then Dad said, "And there's the cemetery. Where your mother is."

I wasn't sure I'd heard him right. Everything went still.

He looked at me closely. "Mardie, I'm sorry I haven't helped you know your mother."

I was so shocked I could barely swallow, much less speak. I couldn't look at him. Instead, I nudged the candy wrappers and cigarette butts with the toe of my shoe. Deer and rabbit poop littered the ground like boxes of spilled Milk Duds and Raisinettes.

Time to be brave. Taking a shaky breath I said, "Tell me about her, Dad. Tell me the good things."

And he did.

We must have sat there like that, side by side, for an hour as he told me about my mother.

He told me about her curiosity, her beauty, her laugh that made everyone else around her laugh. He smiled. "She was so full of life, so dramatic. When I met your mother, it was like that scene in *The Wizard of Oz* where everything suddenly changes from black and white to Technicolor." He looked down at his hands and said, "I could never figure out why she latched on to someone like me."

"Opposites attract?" I offered.

He nodded. "I think you're right. People often seek in another person what they feel they themselves lack."

I drew back in mock surprise. Dad the psychologist?

He chuckled. "Well, that's what Amy says, anyway."

Then in a more serious voice he said, "But I think there's truth in that, too, especially when you're younger. I needed the impulsiveness and daring of your mother that I didn't have. Among other things."

"And what do you think you had she needed?" I asked.

"Stability," he said without hesitating. "Your mom had a rough childhood. Her folks died when she was ten. She didn't have any brothers or sisters. She was bounced around from one relative to another, each worse than the last. By the time she graduated high school, she'd lived in seven different states."

He gazed at the storm clouds building over the mountains. "She wanted stability and the chance to create her own family. I wanted a family, too, and well, I'm nothing if not stable, so . . ." His voice trailed off.

My heart felt heavy. Why did the family have to end, if they both wanted it so much?

Just when I thought he wasn't going to say anything more, he said, "Unfortunately, sometimes what attracts us most to a person in the beginning drives us crazy later. That's certainly what happened with your mother and me."

I shook my head. "And so you guys got in a fight, she got drunk, and she drove off a bridge."

Dad took my chin in his hand and turned my face. "Look at me, Mardie," he said.

I raised my wet eyes. His were red, too.

"Yes, we had a fight. A big fight. I'll never forgive myself for some of the things I said. And yes, she had too much to drink and should never have gotten behind the wheel of a car. But she did. It was winter, we'd had snow earlier. She hit an icy patch and lost control of the car. She was killed instantly. She never knew what happened."

Blinking back tears I said, "Where was she going?"

He dropped his hand from my face. Staring out over our little town he said, "Home. She was coming home."

The whole scene spun out in my head. The fight, the harsh words that could never be taken back; the smoky bar, drink after drink dulling the pain, hoping for more courage. The resolve, finally to go home, to do . . . what? What was she going to do? Make up with Dad, or tell him to go to hell? Was she coming back for us? For me?

As if reading my thoughts, Dad said, "I can't tell you how often I've wondered what she was going to do when she got home. The guilt I felt was almost too much to handle. I beat myself up for a long time with all the what ifs and maybes. If I hadn't had you kids to look after, I don't think I would have made it." He looked at me. "You have so many of her good qualities, Mardie. You have your mother's great laugh, her passion, her determination. You know, she loved horses, too. And like you, she would take on anyone who messed with her friends or her family."

"You mean we aren't both screwups?"

He took both my hands in his. He held them so tight I had to look at him. "You listen to me, young lady," he said. "Your mother was *not* a screwup and neither are you. You and I have had some hard times with each other and I haven't been the perfect father, but I couldn't be more proud of you." In a gentler voice, he said, "And I have no doubt that were your mother alive today, she'd be proud of you, too."

Bumping my shoulder against his, I said, "Thanks, Dad."

He ruffled my hair. "Still not too sure about this new look, though."

I felt like one of those scrub jays, running back down the hill, skimming low above the sagebrush, light and quick.

I felt like I could run from one end of our little town to another, yelling at the top of my lungs, *My dad's proud of me!*

But I didn't. I slowed myself to match my pace to his, breathing his rhythm. I wanted to run home with my dad.

Dad and I burst threw the front door, laughing and arguing.

"I could have gone faster that last mile," Dad said. "I was going easy on you."

"No way," I laughed. "I thought I'd have to call an ambulance."

My cell phone rang. I grabbed it off the coffee table. Rick.

"Hey," I said.

"Want to go to a movie later?" he said.

I ran through my homework in my head. All caught up for once.

"Sure," I said. I watched Dad and Amy slow dance in the kitchen. "Why don't you come by here and we'll take the bus."

TWENTY-ONE

The anger and pain that had fueled my fighting were gone. I was left with passion and curiosity. Passion to be the best I could be, to feel the focus, the control over my body. Curiosity to see just how far I could take it. Just how good I could be. I didn't *need* to be the best, I *wanted* to be the best.

I won my next two matches hands down.

Pueblo was a breeze. The girl I boxed was uncertain, inexperienced. I almost felt sorry for her. But not too much.

Amy and Michael were there to see my first win. Dad, too. Amy was so excited you would have thought I'd won a gold medal at the Olympics. Michael just kept grinning and saying, "Impressive."

Dad, on the other hand, looked like *he* had been the one in the ring with me. "I'm proud of you, Mardie," he said. "But that was hard to watch." All right, so Dad would never enjoy watching me box the way he enjoyed watching Michael play lacrosse.

"That's okay, Dad," I said. And it really was.

The next match two weeks later was in Cottonwood

Creek. For such a small town they had a surprisingly strong boxing club. The girls were well coached and hungry to win.

I still won my match (so did Shireen and Destiny), but I had to work for it—hard. When I shook that girl's hand at the end of the match, she grinned and said, "See you in Denver."

Dad wasn't there for that match. Michael had agreed to play the last lacrosse game of his high school career, and probably his whole life, so Dad went to his game. I did feel a little sad when I looked up in the bleachers and didn't see him there. But Amy was there, cheering louder than anyone else. Who would have thought a librarian could be so rowdy?

School was winding down for the summer and it looked like I was going to finish the year with grades that were actually respectable.

Rick and I spent more and more time together, despite my training. No, he's not as handsome or as dangerous in that exciting kind of way like Ben. But he's a good guy.

Most importantly, though, I felt released, unburdened. I still missed my mom, but in a weird way, I had her now, too. It's like before, what I felt was the *absence* of her. Now I just felt her.

And then there was Alexis.

I hadn't seen much of her since the pregnancy test. The last time I saw her, she and Sam were having an all-time yelling match in the parking lot after school. She wasn't at school the next day.

I tried calling her that weekend, but as usual, she didn't call me back.

Wednesday rolled around, and Thursday came and went, without any word from her. On Friday afternoon, when I was coming back from running with the dogs, I saw her mom working out in their front yard. I screwed up my courage and stopped. "Hey, Mrs. T. Is Alexis home?"

She straightened up from the plants she was trimming and put her hand up, shielding her eyes from the sun. "Oh hi, Mardie," she said. "She is, but she's not feeling well." I expected her to say that I should go on in and cheer her up but she didn't. She just stood there looking like she wished I'd leave.

I wasn't going to give up yet. "So . . . can I go in and see her? Maybe I—"

"I'm not sure that's a good idea right now," she said, cutting me off. This was too weird.

"Okay, well, will you tell her I stopped by and to call me?"

She brushed at her cheek with the back of her hand. "I will, Mardie," she said. "When she's feeling better."

Alexis wasn't at school the next week either. I looked for her in the halls, in the cafeteria. No sign of my friend. I did see Sam, though, hanging out with Ben, Eric, and Megan. What a bunch of losers.

After school on Tuesday, I tried to corner Sam away from the others to find out about Alexis. He just blew me off with a wave of his hand and a "Just be cool, Mardie." Cool my ass.

I was smoldering when I got to the gym that night. I pounded the heavy bag, imagining it was Sam hanging there, then Ben, and then Eric. Just as I was about to step into a kidney punch, Kitty came up behind the bag, stopping its sway. I pulled up short, heart pounding.

"You got the fire in your belly tonight, missy. Wouldn't want to be the person that bag represents."

"People," I corrected her. "Of the male persuasion."

She laughed and shook her head. "Well, let's take that fury of yours over to the ring and put it to good use."

As Kitty laced up my gloves, she said, "Time to take your sparring up another notch."

I looked around. Destiny wasn't there that night and neither was Shireen. "Who will I train with?"

Pulling a pair of gloves out of her duffle bag, she said, "Me."

I was dumbstruck. I knew Kitty boxed professionally at one time. I'd seen the trophies in her office. But for some reason, I never thought of her *in* the ring.

Reading the surprise on my face, she said, "It only makes sense, Mardie. You're way better than Shireen now. She's good enough, but she's not going to give you a challenge.

"I think you've got a decent shot to win in Denver," Kitty continued. "But if you want to do more than just show up, we got to take you to the next level. And the person to take you there is yours truly."

"But what about Destiny? She always makes me work hard in the ring. I learn a lot from her. Why can't I just spar with her from now on?"

Kitty waved a gloved hand in my face. "Listen to yourself, Mardie," she said. "It's all me, me, me. Well, it's not all *about* you!"

I flinched.

"Listen, Destiny wants to not only win in Denver, she wants to go pro. And she can. But she, just like you, needs to take her training up over the next month. Quite frankly, sparring with you won't do her any favors."

"So is she going to train with you, too?" I asked.

Standing up, stretching her long arms over her head, she said, "Naw. I've taught her all my tricks. She's going to be training with Roberto."

I was totally shocked. "*Roberto Molleta?* But," I stammered, "he's a *guy*!"

Kitty laughed as she ducked under the ropes. "You noticed, huh?"

Roberto Molleta wasn't just a guy, he was a very cool, *very* hot guy. He was also an amazingly talented boxer. He coached the guys on Monday and Wednesday nights. I'd seen him working with some of them on open night. He'd even won several professional fights. But Destiny?

Kitty winked. "Just between you and me, I know for a fact he's had his eye on Destiny for a long time. He's more than happy to have an excuse to spend a little time with her."

Destiny?

"Guess it's just like my mom always said: 'There's a lid for every pot.'" Punching me in the arm, she said, "Now, let's get down to work."

Most everyone had gone home. The lights were off except for the bright lights over the ring. Once we both pulled our headgear on, got our mouthpieces in, and locked eyes on each other, there was nothing else.

There was no tournament, no jerky guys, no disappearing friends, no dead mothers, no disappointing fathers, and no apologies. There was just me and Kitty and boxing. It was pure, and it was fun.

And it was also work. Kitty may have called me "missy" outside of the ring, may have hugged me and joked with me, but in the ring, she was all business. And speed and calculation.

Some of my jabs just glanced off her headgear, others she slipped with ease. But I will say I got some very satisfying jabs and right crosses in, and a body shot that rattled her. But she shook it off and danced away. We circled each other, our breathing synchronized. Jab, dance, breathe. Watch the eyes, how she moves her head. Slip that cross. Focus. Dance. Breathe.

Alexis came back to school, pale as winter.

During our lunch break, I coaxed her from the cafeteria to the bright sun of the outside commons area. We sat on the warm concrete, our backs leaning against sun-warmed walls. She closed her eyes, tipped her head back. I had a million questions I wanted to ask her.

"So, where have you *been*, Alexis?"

Maybe she wasn't going to answer. But then she said, "Home. In bed."

"Why?"

She sighed. "Let's just say I'm a failure at guys and at life in general."

"I hear you," I said. It wasn't that long ago I felt the same way.

She looked at me. "Yeah, I guess you would know. Sam and I got into a big fight. We broke up. Everything felt like it was crashing in, you know?"

Boy, did I.

"I found out from one of the girls in Drama Club that he'd been hooking up with another girl in Drama Club. One I thought was my friend." Alexis shook her head. "Guess she wasn't."

"It totally sucks," I said.

She nodded. "So disappearing seemed like a good idea. At the time."

She looked at me with eyes that tried to smile, but couldn't. "I took a whole bottle of aspirin, along with a bunch of vodka."

"Oh, my god, Alexis."

"The only thing *that* got me was a trip to the emergency room and two sessions a week with a shrink."

I took her hand.

She sighed. "The weird part is, I don't feel anything. I know there's a lot of things I should feel, but I don't."

I wanted to punch something. Or someone. Several, in fact. I told her, and for the first time, she sort of laughed.

"Maybe boxing would be good for me, too. Might feel good to beat up something—other than myself."

"Trust me, it does," I said. "You could come with me Thursday night."

"Well, well, well," a low, raspy voice purred. "If it isn't

my two favorite losers." The sun backlit a head of magenta hair.

Alexis pressed herself against the wall, trying to disappear.

"What's up, Megan?" I stood up and tried my best to look bored or annoyed. But if she'd started in on Alexis, I was going to take her head off.

A look of momentary confusion flashed across her face. She wasn't expecting something that straightforward.

She picked at something under one of her chipped fingernails. "Figured where there's smoke, there's fire."

"Meaning what?" I asked.

Still not really looking at us, she said, "Just wondering if you've seen Sam or Eric."

I shrugged. "Can't help you there. Alexis and I aren't exactly on their top-ten list of people to hang with. They're probably somewhere killing off what few brain cells they have left."

"Or getting beat up by girls," Alexis added.

"Or fags," I said, smiling.

"Or vegans," Alexis snorted. We looked at each other and burst out laughing. I held my sides because they still ached from sparring with Kitty. Alexis howled, hands pressed to her face. Tears streamed down her cheeks.

Megan looked at us, shook her head, and left. The bell rang. I helped Alexis to her feet.

"Let's get you to class," I said.

She didn't let go of my hand.

"Better watch it," I said. "People are going to think you're a dyke."

She grinned. "Who the hell cares?"

TWENTY-TWO

Tuesday night at the gym. Four days before D-Day. "I've gotten some preliminary information from Denver," Kitty said. Butterflies swooped through my stomach.

She handed each of us an information sheet. "This tells you how to find Skyline High School, where the tournament will be held. Opening ceremonies will be from ten-thirty to eleven. The first bouts in the five weight divisions will begin at eleven-thirty, probably go until five. You'll have the night to recuperate, then the finals will run most of the day on Sunday." The finals. Would I even make it that far?

"How many girls will be there?" Destiny asked.

"I heard there will be about thirty girls. But there's always some no-shows."

I was disappointed. "Only *thirty*?" I said. "I thought there were supposed to be girls coming from all over the Rockies."

Kitty shrugged. "Not all of the states in the region *have* girls' clubs. In years past, it's mostly been Colorado, Idaho, and Utah that have been represented. Still, we get a few more girls every year. Nothing like back East," she said. "But it's getting better."

Shireen and I waited out front for Amy. Shireen was nervous, fidgety. "I'm just not ready for this, *chica*. It seemed like such a good idea back in December, you know?"

Totally.

Trying to make her feel better, I said, "It's our first time to regionals. We're just going to check things out, see what it's like. You know what Kitty said: hardly anyone ever wins their division the first time."

But I felt as ready as I was ever going to be. Over the past month, I'd trained harder than I ever thought I could. Dad arranged for me to do interval training with the track team at the college. I wasn't sure I wanted to take time away from my long runs, but after just a few workouts with the track team, my legs were amazingly stronger, and quicker. Kitty and I trained every day for two hours: weights, jump roping, heavy bag, and speed bag.

And of course, lots of time in the ring. It took some getting used to, Kitty fighting me *and* training me at the same time. We worked so hard, I'd hear her in my sleep.

"Move those feet, Mardie! Move!" "Hook it! Hook it!" "Watch my eyes, not my hands! Never the hands!" "Hands up, chin tucked. Don't be afraid to move inside!"

I'd wake up exhausted. I promised myself if I got out of Denver alive, I'd do nothing all summer but lie on the couch and watch reruns of *CSI*.

So I was thinking about all this the next afternoon as I waited for Dad to pick me up from the track. Intervals and sprints with the track team had kicked my butt. I was ready to go home.

I sprawled in the grass at the edge of the field stretching my hamstrings, oblivious to the world when—

"Alone at last." I looked over my shoulder. Eric Lindstrom towered over me.

Every instinct, every fiber in my body demanded I fight or run. In a matter of seconds, though, my brain sized up the situation: If I ran, he'd get me before I even got off the ground. He'd pulverize me if I fought him, but maybe I'd at least break his nose again.

Then I heard Kitty's voice say, "Use your brains, not your fists."

Eric took a step closer, his fists clenching and unclenching. "Just you and me, babe. I been dreaming of this moment."

I forced myself to look relaxed. "I'm flattered you dream about me, Eric."

"I'm about to become your worst nightmare," he said. "After I teach you a lesson."

"And that lesson would be?" I asked, hoping to buy some time, hoping to see Dad's car any second.

"A lesson in keeping your smart-ass mouth under control."

"That's nice, Eric, for you to make such a sacrifice for someone like me."

He snorted a snarky kind of snort. "I'm not making any 'sacrifice' for you, bitch. I'm doing you a favor by—"

I held up my hand. "Oh but you are. Sacrificing, I mean. Not only are you sacrificing valuable time and energy dreaming of teaching me these lessons, you're willing to sacrifice your *future* to do it."

Eric looked truly puzzled.

"Let's say you do 'teach me a lesson' right here and now, and beat the holy crap out of me. And I'm not kidding myself, Eric. I know you could."

He nodded. "You got that right."

I nodded, too, my mouth full of cotton. "Yeah so, you'd beat the crap out of me. My dad, who's due here any second, finds me, bloody mess and all. And you'd end up in prison for beating up a fifteen-year-old girl."

He shrugged. "He'd never know it was me."

I sighed, even though I felt like I was having a heart attack. "Like you said, Eric, I got a big mouth. You'd have to kill me to shut me up."

His eyes went cold and hard. *Where was Dad?*

"And even if you did that," I continued, "everyone would know."

"Oh really," he said.

"Yep," I said. "One of the things I hate about living in a small town is *everyone* knows your business."

A car came around the side of the field house. It drew closer. My heart fell. It wasn't Dad. *Shit.*

Eric's eyes followed my gaze. A lightbulb went off in my brain.

The red BMW convertible pulled into the parking lot. This was my chance. I stood and waved.

"There's my dad," I said. "Mr. Punctual."

I swung my backpack on one shoulder. I smiled, hoping Eric wouldn't notice my knees shaking. I also prayed the little red car wouldn't pull away. I waved again to whomever was in the car.

I patted Eric's arm. "Good talking with you, Eric." He jerked away like he'd been burned. "Have a great life." I turned and tried my best to saunter away.

"Fuck you, you crazy bitch," he said to my back.

My smart-ass self wanted to have the last in-your-face word. But I practiced monumental self-control. I focused on walking away from Eric without a word.

Halfway to the parking lot, I saw a beautiful sight: my dad's boring, practical, tan Honda Civic driving toward me. I waved like a maniac.

TWENTY-THREE

It was finally time to leave for Denver. Amy spent most of the evening packing food, drinks, pillows, and blankets for the trip. You'd think we were driving to Outer Mongolia instead of a major city. She asked me for the millionth time as I tried to sneak past her in the kitchen, "You have all your gear packed? Your suitcase for the motel?"

"Geez, Amy," I groaned. "Give it a rest, would you? I'm all packed. We've done this a few times, you know."

"I know, but we've always come right back from the match. This time we're staying over. You'll need more stuff. I just want to make sure—"

Thank god, right at that moment Michael wandered into the kitchen. She pounced on him with, "And what about you, young man?"

Michael looked at me, then at Amy. "What about me?"

I laughed as I grabbed a soda out of the fridge. "You're in for it now." We'd take Michael to the airport for his flight to Europe the day after the championship. Michael groaned as Amy said, "Let's just go up to your room and go through your stuff one more time. I made this list . . ."

As I packed the last of my stuff in my duffle, my cell phone rang.

"Hey Mardie, it's Alexis."

"Hey yourself," I said, trying to decide which pair of jeans were the least trashed.

"I just wanted to thank you for being such a good friend."

I frowned. "What's up with you? Did you find religion or something?"

Alexis laughed. "Yeah, think I'll join a convent."

"Hey, that reminds me," I said, deciding on my favorite pair of jeans with the double pockets on the back. "You still owe me nineteen bucks for that home pregnancy test."

Alexis sighed. I pictured her curling up in her huge beanbag chair. "God, that was all so stupid."

"And scary," I said.

"Scared the virginity right back into me," she said.

I laughed. It felt good to have Alexis making me laugh again.

"Anyway, Mar," she said. "I just wanted to say you're a good friend and I hope you kick ass in Denver."

"I just want to come back in one piece," I said.

"You'll be awesome," she said. "Totally."

The drive to Denver was long and boring. Shireen was riding with her whole family; Kitty and Destiny and Roberto were in another car.

I just wanted to get there, get on with that first bout. If

I could get that first one over with, and better yet *win it*, the rest would be a piece of cake.

As we walked toward the entrance to the gym, I heard the school band warming up and cheerleaders practicing cheers.

"You've got to be kidding," a voice said behind me. "Cheerleaders at a boxing tournament?"

"Hey!" I threw my arms around Shireen.

A tall, absolutely gorgeous woman strode up behind Shireen. "You forgot your mouthpiece, *chica*," she said.

She smiled at Amy and Dad. "She doesn't usually forget things. Guess she's excited."

Dad smiled and stuck out his hand. "I'm Dave Wolfe, Mardie's father and the nervous parent here."

"I'm Shireen's mom, Marsella Avenado," she said, laughing. "And I'm a proud member of the Nervous Parent Club, too."

I introduced Michael. "And this is my mom, Amy Bayne," I said.

Amy shook Mrs. Avenado's hand. "Well, stepmother. I'm not her real mother."

I slipped my arm around her shoulders, saying, "You're as real as they get." And you know what, I realized for the first time that it was true.

"Girls, let's go," Kitty called from the locker rooms.

We left the families and hurried across the gym. "I thought your sibs were coming, too," I said.

"Nah," Shireen said. "Mama decided she didn't want them seeing me get beat up, so they're staying with Grandma."

"That's too bad."

"It's okay," she said as Kitty swept us into the locker room. "I can't remember the last time I had my mom all to myself. It'll be kind of nice."

"Hit the locker room and get changed, girls," Kitty said.

It went quick from there. Weigh-in, doc check, equipment check. Then all the boxers paraded out to the bleachers at the far end of the gym.

The opening ceremonies were really lame, but kind of sweet, too. I mean, they were trying so hard! From the girl who couldn't quite hit that high note in the national anthem, to the band trying to sound really jazzy playing the theme song from *Rocky*, to the cheerleaders bouncing around, chanting at the tops of their pretty little lungs, "Two, four, six, eight! Here's the best boxers in the state! Colorado! Idaho! Utah!"

I scanned the bleachers to get a better look at the other girl fighters. Idaho may have had the smallest team, but they had the coolest uniforms: electric-blue satin shirts with black skulls printed on them. Seemed like there must have been a law that you had to be blond to be on the Utah team. They all looked so perky-sweet.

At the end, we all stood up, state by state, and waved to the crowd. I'll have to admit, it was pretty damn awesome to hear all those people cheering and whistling.

"Gather 'round, girls," Kitty said, back in our corner of the locker room. She had the clipboard in her hand with the day's roster of bouts. "Mardie, the bantam-weight division is first since it's the smallest weight classification. Including you, there are eight girls in your division."

"Holy crap," Shireen said. "Does she have to fight them all to win?"

I was thinking the same thing. "No," Kitty said. "You'll be paired up based on experience. You'll each have two matches today, that is, if you win your first one. The winners of today's matches will go on to the finals tomorrow."

I couldn't even think about tomorrow.

"Shireen, you're in the feather-weight division. That's the biggest division."

"And how many is that?" Shireen asked nervously. Kitty consulted her clipboard. "Looks like ten, including you."

Shireen groaned. "I am *so* screwed."

"Destiny, you're in the light welter weight division." Destiny nodded. "How many?"

Kitty shook her head. "Pretty small field. Only six." Destiny looked shocked. "Including me?"

"Including you. They'll be good bouts, I'm sure."

I pawed through my gym bag looking for my mouthpiece. Shireen paced back and forth. She'd pace from one side of the locker room to the other, come back, sit beside me, jump up, and pace some more. Finally, when she sat down by me for the millionth time, I grabbed her arm. "Stay. Put."

Her mouth worked her chewing gum like a jackhammer. "I just don't feel ready for this, do you?"

I shrugged.

"I mean, this is big-time. This isn't like fighting country girls just up the road," she said.

"No," I said. "It isn't."

She looked at me with eyes like a bunny in the headlights. "Then what the heck are we doing here, Mardie?"

I put an arm around her shoulders. "Because Kitty believes in us. And our folks believe in us, and we believe in us." I gave her a little shake. "Right?"

"Boxers to the ring, please!" I would hear that from the announcer several times that weekend. And every time I heard it, I felt like I was going to pee in my blue satin shorts.

Thankfully, my first bout was a piece of cake. When the girl from Idaho and I touched gloves at center ring, I saw two things that made me feel good: doubt in her eyes and arms much shorter than mine. She'd never have the reach to get me inside, and I'd mess with her head. Feed her doubt.

Which is exactly what I did. I came out confident, leading with a strong right jab, easily batting away her attempts to work her way inside. By the end of the third round, I'd out-pointed her 18-9. My first win.

"Great match," the girl from Idaho said. We hugged after the judges' decision was announced. I felt awesome. I'd made it to the afternoon round.

Basking in the glow of my win, I went back to the locker room to give Shireen some moral support.

Kitty wrapped her hands, talking to her in a low, soothing voice. I could see why. Both legs jiggled up and down. She was hyperventilating.

"Save your energy, Shireen," Kitty kept saying over and over.

Shireen looked around the room wildly, noticing me for the first time. "Great match, Mardie!" she said, her smile more like a grimace. "You were awesome!"

I walked behind her, massaged wire-tight shoulders. "You'll do great, too," I said.

But she didn't hear me. Instead, she asked Kitty in a whiny little-kid voice, "Why aren't you using the blue wraps? You know I do best with the blue wraps."

Kitty tried to talk her down. "Don't you worry. I have your blue wraps," she said. "But you have to have gauze first." Wrapping the ten feet of gauze over and over Shireen's hand in her own intricate pattern, Kitty reminded her, "The announcer will call you to the ring. You'll be in the blue corner. You'll touch gloves with your opponent and the ref will explain the rules."

Shireen nodded, snapping her gum and tapping one mummy hand on her thigh.

"When the bell rings," Kitty continued, "you come out and fight. If the girl hits you first, don't worry about it. Just keep your hands up and concentrate on those killer combinations of yours. The judges want to see combos rather than straight punches."

Kitty pulled the big leather mitts from her equipment bag. "Let's hit the mitts a little bit, Shireen. Get your energy focused."

"I'll hit with her," I said.

Kitty shook her head, frowning. She nodded toward Shireen, bouncing up and down on the balls of her feet like a maniac. "She's too wild, Mardie," she said. "Don't want to take the chance of you getting hurt."

Shireen won her first bout, barely. Her opponent, a black girl from the Denver boxing club, had a definite height and reach advantage. Shireen's work during the first round was wild and unfocused. The Denver girl took advantage by backing her up to the corner. Shireen caught her with a combination, but didn't follow up. And she didn't counter at all.

"Crap," Destiny said. "She's not going to survive the first round." I couldn't believe it, either. It was like Shireen had given up. She was just trying to hang in there until the end of the round.

Destiny slipped behind the judges' table, made her way over to Kitty. She said something in Kitty's ear. Kitty nodded, not taking her eyes off Shireen.

Finally, the bell signaled the end of the first round. Shireen slumped on her stool, eyes closed as Kitty removed her mouthpiece and squirted water into her mouth. Kitty was talking fast and furious to her. Shireen just kept shaking her head. I figured she might as well just retire from the match and call it a day.

But then I saw Shireen stiffen, look at Kitty like she had just called her the worst thing possible. Fury colored her face. Seconds after the bell rang for the second round and Shireen stood up, it was clear *la chica loca* was back. The girl from Denver never knew what hit her.

Destiny's bout ended after the first round. It was clear to everyone in the gym that despite the fact that Destiny was a good three inches shorter than the girl from Utah, she was the superior boxer. In her cold, methodical way, she took the girl apart. It was so one-sided I almost felt sorry for the tall redhead.

The bell rang ending the first round. Then much to my surprise, after talking with the judges, the ref came back to the center of the ring and announced Destiny the winner by a 16-5 point spread.

"It's over?" I asked.

"Yeah," Roberto said, grinning. "It's called the 'mercy rule'. Bouts are stopped at the end of a round if one of the boxers is at least ten points ahead of their opponent. That girl didn't have a prayer of catching our Destiny." His beautiful face glowed with pride.

My second bout was harder than the morning match, but I still won 20-17.

Shireen was still channeling *la chica loca*. I think she scared her opponent to death.

And Destiny's opponent, a powerfully built Latina from the Denver club, was the second to succumb to the mercy rule. All three of us were set for the finals the next day.

Dad, Amy, Michael, and Shireen's mom waded down through the spectators from the seats in the bleachers and found us in the crowd on the floor.

Michael flung one long arm around my shoulder and gave me a hard squeeze. "You made me proud today, little sister. You were sweet out there!" He even hugged Shireen (I've never seen her blush so hard) and shook Destiny's hand. "Amazing! Just amazing!" he kept saying as he pumped her hand.

Amy was so excited, I thought she was going to pee in *her* pants. "You did it!" she cried, hugging me to the point of suffocation. "I am *so proud of you!*" Turning and hugging Shireen *and* Destiny in one swoop, she said, "All of you! I'm so proud of *all* of you!"

Untangling herself from Amy's embrace, Destiny said, "Thank you, Mrs. Wolfe, but we still have tomorrow to go."

Dad looked like he'd been through ten rounds. His face was drawn and tired, his eyes still wearing that "worried parent" look. Still, he hugged me close and said, "I'm proud of you, too, bug."

After we all had dinner that night, I crashed. I stretched out on the huge king-sized bed in my motel room and flipped through the endless channels on TV. Nothing. I wished Shireen were sharing a room with me so we could talk. But she and her mom were having girl time.

I flipped open my cell phone and punched in the numbers. He picked up on the first ring.

"Hey," Rick said. "How did it go today? Are you okay? You didn't get hurt, did you?"

I laughed and curled into the mountain of pillows. "I miss you, too."

"I do miss you," he said. "I wish I were there right now."

Little fish danced in my veins. "What would you do if you were here?"

"Watch you," he said. "Just watch you."

I yawned. "I'm afraid you'd be pretty bored."

"One thing you will never be, Mardie Wolfe, is boring."

Twenty-Four

The parking lot of the high school filled up early the next morning. Trucks with satellite dishes perched on top, news logos emblazoned on the sides, lined the NO PARKING zones.

"Guess you're newsworthy, little sister," Michael said.

It was oddly quiet in the locker room. Normally, you get twelve girls together in a room and it's party time. Everybody teasing and laughing and singing.

Not today. Some girls talked quietly together, others were silent as their coaches wrapped their hands. Some even looked like they were meditating. Or praying. Destiny, as usual, sat alone with her Sudoku books.

Kitty motioned us over to a corner where she'd set up shop. "I want to talk with you both before we get busy with all the weigh-ins and stuff." She sounded way too serious.

Shireen looked at me anxiously. I shrugged and sat on a bench across from Kitty.

"Today is going to be a different ball game, ladies. Today you are competing against the best of the best. And you two are among them." She leaned forward, fixing us with her intense stare. "I didn't expect either of you to go this far."

"Geez, Kitty," I said. "You sure know how to make a girl feel *good*."

"What I am trying to say is you have far exceeded my expectations for this tournament. I would've been happy if you'd only won one bout yesterday. But instead you both took the whole shootin' match."

"Isn't today the 'shootin' match'?" I asked.

Kitty finally smiled. "Today, missy, is icing on the cake. Today is *gravy*."

Shireen looked confused. "But don't you want us to win?"

"What I want is for you two to be *proud* of yourselves. You both set the goal six months ago of coming to this tournament. You both had plenty of reasons to give up on that goal, but you didn't. You trained hard, physically and mentally. You stuck with it even when other people tried to tear you down."

She grasped both of our hands hard. "Don't ever forget what this feels like, to believe in yourself. To be *proud* of who you are."

Giving our hands a final squeeze, she said, "Today is about fun, girlfriends! You got nothing to prove to nobody, so go out there and have fun with it."

Shireen still didn't look too sure about this, but my insides were light as a handful of feathers.

My first bout was with the girl I'd beaten in Cottonwood last month. She was out for revenge.

I had a tough time with her the first round. She just

wouldn't back off, and she'd developed a mean left hook since I'd last fought her.

The second round wasn't any easier. We both came out landing hard punches, neither of us willing to retreat.

"Get her inside," Destiny called from the sidelines.

I tried my best to work her against the ropes. She slipped my uppercut and danced away, just out of reach. Damn.

The bell rang.

"She's killing me," I said to Kitty.

"She's tough," Kitty said, wiping the sweat from my face. "But you've beaten her before. You can do it again."

"But—"

The bell rang.

"You can do this, Mardie. She's weak on her left. Take advantage of it."

I pulled all my focus into one fine point and unleashed the heat. I moved in with a quick uppercut and jab combo. She threw a head shot, but her glove glanced off my headgear. Kitty was right. She never fully used her left side.

I faked with my right shoulder and caught her with a left jab, followed with my signature hook.

Her eyes widened. She stumbled. The match was all mine.

The bell rang, ending the final round. I won a 24-20 decision. As we hugged center ring, she said, grinning, "We need to do this more often."

I laughed. The girl had style.

Shireen lost her match that morning. As Destiny said later, it just wasn't in the cards for her to win this time around. When the announcer said she was fighting the reigning Rocky Mountain Feather-weight Champion, we knew it was all over.

To her credit, though, she did go all three rounds. Wiping the sweat away from her swollen eye, she said, "At least they didn't have to pull that mercy rule on me."

Destiny's morning opponent won the award for most bizarre prebout behavior. She danced around her corner, pumping her arms and strutting like a rooster.

"Looks like that girl's taken too many shots to the head," Roberto grumbled.

Then, much to our amusement and the ref's astonishment, she lowered her head and pawed the canvas with her foot like a bull ready to charge. She was crazy.

"Uh, uh, uh," Kitty muttered. "Destiny's goin' to take care of that girl's business."

And she did. By the middle of the second round, Bull Girl was down and the ref was doing the eight count.

After a one-hour lunch break came the final bouts.

"I'm *glaaaad* I'm out of the running, girlfriend," Shireen kept singing over and over while she stuffed a cheeseburger and a huge plate of fries in her mouth.

Her mother shook her head. "Frankly, I'm glad, too," she said to Dad.

All I could manage was a protein shake Amy brought me and some almonds. I tried to drink a soda, but it made me too jittery.

And then, all too soon, the announcer said one last time, "Boxers to the ring, please!"

"And now, ladies and gentlemen, the final match of the women's bantam-weight division!"

The crowd cheered and whistled. The taste of almonds burned my throat.

"In the red corner, weighing in at 119 pounds, the reigning bantam-weight champion . . . "

I looked up at Kitty. "Reigning champion? Did he say reigning champion?"

Kitty patted my shoulder.

What the hell am I doing here?

While the ref recited the rules we all knew by heart, she looked me up and down. Her lip curled as best it could around her mouthpiece. In all honesty, it was a pretty impressive sneer.

When we touched gloves, she managed to say, "You're meat."

I almost swallowed my mouthpiece.

The bell rang. "Go get her, Mardie," Kitty said.

The Queen strode out of her corner.

I'd test her, see where her weakness was. Play with her a little, then—

Slam! A block of concrete hit me just under the eye, followed by a sledgehammer to the jaw.

I staggered back, working my jaw back and forth.

"Get in there, Mardie!" someone called.

I threw my gloves up in front of my face. The Queen dropped her right hand to nail my ribs. Just enough of an opening for me to hook her with a left.

Her eyes widened with surprise, then turned hard as glass. She charged in with a flurry of jabs.

Just as she was about to work me against the rope, the bell rang.

I slumped on the hard wooden stool. Sweat poured down my back. Every inch of my body screamed in pain.

Who did I think I was, thinking I could win a boxing championship? That creepy voice whispered, *Freak. Loser.*

I closed my eyes as Kitty squirted cool water on my bruised lips. Water trickled down my throat. She talked fast and furious in my ear, but I didn't hear her or see her.

Instead, I saw Hannah and Roger and Lizzie, and Alexis and my mother, all of us trying our best to just be who we are. No apologies.

I opened my eyes and searched the stands for Dad. I spotted him, his eyes fixed on me. Yes, he looked worried, but he also looked proud.

Our eyes locked for one instant, brief as a shooting star. We both smiled.

The bell rang for the last round. Kitty popped my mouthpiece in. "It's all gravy, girlfriend."

I nodded. Win, lose, or draw, it didn't matter. *I, Mardie Wolfe, am good enough.*

I danced forward, light as a feather.

The Queen sauntered out of her corner, smirking around her mouthpiece again. *She thinks she's got this sucker won.*

I crouched, keeping my elbows in, letting my arms take the body shots. I lured her into a false sense of security. Sure enough, she let down her guard. I stepped in, peppered her with a flurry of counterpunches, working my way inside. I looked in her eyes and saw frustration and the slightest edge of fear.

That was my signal.

I nailed her with a hard body shot, feinted left with my head, and popped her with a right jab.

The Queen staggered.

I moved in quickly for the kill. I hit her with all my best combinations, praying that one of them would work.

But there was a reason she was undefeated for two years.

Before I realized what'd happened, she'd worked me against the ropes. I tucked in, protecting my face and head.

"Get inside, Mardie!" Kitty shouted.

I popped her in the belly. She barely budged. I leaned into her, wrapped my arms around her.

The ref pulled us apart. "No holding," he said. But it gave me room to breathe.

"Stick and run," Kitty called.

Jab, jab. Dance away. Jab.

The Queen panted. Our world was reduced to our breath, our eyes locked on each other, and what we both wanted.

Out of nowhere, her fist slammed into my head. My mouthpiece flew across the canvas.

I fell to my knees, trying not to puke.

Just as the ref started the eight count, the bell rang.

It was over.

The ref pulled me to my feet, walked me to the center of the ring. The Queen and I looped our arms around each other's waists, awaiting the decision.

She squeezed me and said out of the side of her mouth, "You are one tough girl fighter."

The ref returned with that white piece of paper in his hands. "The winner by a 23-18 decision, in the red trunks, the reigning bantam-weight champion—"

I leaned into her ear. "Enjoy it, because this is your last year," I said.

I looked up in the stands. Amy, Michael, and Dad waved a huge banner. I threw back my head and laughed. The banner read: DON'T MESS WITH THE WOLFE!!

I blew them a kiss with my bruised lips, long skinny arms, and huge, gloved hands.

EPILOGUE

The road out to the quarry is dusty this time of year. It's only mid-June but it's already hot and dry. I run past pastures turning from emerald green to a tired-looking shade of its former self. My running shoes kick up little puffs of dirt as I trot along, three miles into an eight miler.

Okay, so I don't seem to be taking the summer off, laying on the couch watching reruns. But I did take a couple of weeks off to let my body heal and to come back down from the incredible high of the tournament. I wanted to savor it as long as I could. There will never be anything like that feeling of standing up there on the podium with the other first- and second-place winners of their divisions.

Just like in the Olympics, one of the judges slipped a silver medal over my head, handed me a bouquet of flowers, and shook my hand. I always thought it was pretty lame the way the athletes in the Olympics cried when they heard their country's national anthem. But now I understand because I did the same thing. So did Destiny.

Except we didn't hear the national anthem. Oh no, we got to hear the Skyline High School chorus sing "The Impossible Dream."

It was totally cheesy, but sweet.

I think about the last time I ran down this road. It was cold and raining and I thought my life was over. Hell, I *wanted* it to be over. And all because of a friggin' guy.

I've come a long way on this road.

I am so totally in my head that I don't hear the car come up behind me. I jump to the side, startled.

The window on the driver's side rolls down. A familiar, two-hundred-watt smile.

Shit, shit, shit! I'm thinking to myself. Here I am three miles from anywhere and no one knows where I am. I am so stupid! Why didn't I at least bring the dogs or my cell?

I eye the fields to my left, wondering how fast I can haul my butt across them, when Ben steps out of the sleek, black car and says, "Hey there, Mardie."

I take a deep breath, trying to steady my hammering heart. I say, as casually as I can, "What's happening, Ben? That a new car?"

He looks at the car, almost like he's forgotten he had it. "Oh yeah," he says. "My dad gave it to me for graduation. You like it?"

I can't believe I'm standing here on the old quarry road talking to Ben about his *car*. I manage a smile. "Sure. It's great. That's an awesome present."

He shrugs, then surprises the hell out of me by saying, "Hey, I just wanted to stop and congratulate you on that boxing tournament. That is so cool!"

For a minute I'm confused, thinking, *How the hell does he know?* But then I remember the small photo the newspaper ran in the back of the sports section, a grainy black-and-white picture of me and Dad hugging and holding up my medal. The caption read: LOCAL GIRL, MARDIE WOLFF, MINES SILVER IN DENVER. I have it framed on my dresser next to the picture of my mother.

I laugh and shrug. "My fifteen seconds of fame. They didn't even spell my last name right."

Ben nods. "Still though, it's sweet."

I look him up and down. God, he's still hot. "But you thought it was weird that I boxed."

He looks truly puzzled. "I never said that."

Ben shakes his head. "I mean, I'm not saying I was perfect. I was getting into some stupid shit hanging around with Eric. And well, it did kind of weird me out seeing you up in that ring." Then he switches on that killer smile, spreads his arms wide, and says, "But hey, boys will be boys!"

I shake my head, look down at my dusty running shoes, and laugh.

He looks up the road toward the quarry, then down at a gold watch on his wrist, glinting in the sun. "I'm meeting Megan down at the quarry for a swim." Wiggling his eyebrows he says, "We'll probably go skinny dipping. I got some good weed, too. You want to come out and play, Mardie?"

I shake my head. "Thanks anyway."

He slips into his leather car seat, slams the door shut, and leans out the window. "Okay, well, I just wanted to say congrats, Mardie."

I watch his car disappear down the road and fade away in a cloud of dust. I look up at the hawk still circling lazily over the field. I can't believe my life.

I put the earphones back in and crank up the music.

The road and the whole summer stretch out before me. There will be more intense and wildly fun days training at the gym with Kitty, Destiny, and Shireen. Nationals are coming up late fall in Augusta, Georgia. Dad says if I want to go see what it's like, we'll make a family trip out of it, take some extra time and visit Michael.

But that's a long way away. Right now I just want to spend the summer hanging with my friends.

Alexis is coming to the gym now. Who would have thought someone so small could hit so hard? Kitty calls her Mighty Mouse.

I'll have time to go to New Horizons two days a week. Hannah's new goal is to ride five minutes without anybody holding her. That girl just goes to show you never know where you'll find your real heroes.

And then there's Rick. Thinking of that boy's sweet kisses, I shiver in the summer heat.

I take the turnoff that cuts back toward town and my house and my family. I crank up the iPod and sing right along at the top of my lungs. It just doesn't get any better than this.

ACKNOWLEDGMENTS

Although the writing of a novel is a solitary affair, every writer has a group of patient, good-humored folks who support and encourage them along the way.

I owe bucket-loads of thanks to my amazing editor and friend, Evelyn Fazio. She believed in this book when others didn't, asked all the important questions, and gave me great movie suggestions. I'd also like to thank Susannah Noel, the world's most patient copy editor.

This book would never have seen the light of day without the support and unflinching suggestions from the talented women in my critique group—Chris Graham, Lora Koehler, and Jean Reagan—all gifted writers. I also want to thank my early readers, Claire Reilly-Shapiro, Lisa Actor, and Emma Gavin, for their insight.

The book, *Without Apology: Girls, Women, and the Desire to Fight*, by Leah Hager Cohen provided invaluable insight and inspiration into the world of women's boxing.

Finally and most importantly, I want to thank my husband, Todd. Without his support (emotional, financial, and technical), love, faith, good humor, and most excellent chocolate cookies, I could not have pursued my dream.